P9-DDF-286

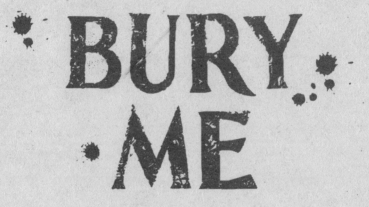

BURY ME

BURY ME

K. R. Alexander

Scholastic Inc.

If you purchased this book without a cover, you should be aware that this book is stolen property. It was reported as "unsold and destroyed" to the publisher, and neither the author nor the publisher has received any payment for this "stripped book."

Copyright © 2019 by Alex R. Kahler writing as K. R. Alexander

All rights reserved. Published by Scholastic Inc., *Publishers since 1920*. scholastic and associated logos are trademarks and/or registered trademarks of Scholastic Inc.

The publisher does not have any control over and does not assume any responsibility for author or third-party websites or their content.

No part of this publication may be reproduced, stored in a retrieval system, or transmitted in any form or by any means, electronic, mechanical, photocopying, recording, or otherwise, without written permission of the publisher. For information regarding permission, write to Scholastic Inc., Attention: Permissions Department, 557 Broadway, New York, NY 10012.

This book is a work of fiction. Names, characters, places, and incidents are either the product of the author's imagination or are used fictitiously, and any resemblance to actual persons, living or dead, business establishments, events, or locales is entirely coincidental.

ISBN 978-1-338-33879-9

10 9 8 7 6 5 4 3 2 1   19 20 21 22 23

Printed in the U.S.A.   40
First printing 2019

Book design by Baily Crawford

For those who seek
to unearth the truth

No one ever leaves Copper Hollow.

No one really questions why. We don't have much, but everything we need is right here. Nothing is great, but nothing is terrible either. Nothing bad ever happens here. It's Copper Hollow. It's always been the same.

Some people might get bored, but not me. Not with my imagination. I can transform any situation into an adventure. I can make even a sleepy old town like Copper Hollow seem exciting. At least, that's what I tell myself. When the summer days are super long, or when I realize that this day feels exactly the same as the one before, I try to use my imagination to make everything new again. Most of the time, it works. There are times, though, when it feels like even my imagination isn't enough.

It's like a part of me is waiting for something. A *real* adventure. A real thrill.

But Copper Hollow never changes. There are no real adventures. No true thrills.

At least, not until the doll appears. Then everything changes.

Maybe I should have tried leaving Copper Hollow earlier . . . while I had a chance.

"Captain Kimberly, our ship is sinking!"

Alicia's voice calls out to me, the cannons firing all around us and the smell of burning wood and sea salt in the air. James is high up in the crow's nest while Alicia fires our own cannons at the Empire's ships and I control the great steering wheel. I survey the many ships around us and shout out their locations to Alicia and James. "Starboard! Three o'clock!" Alicia tries to follow my commands, tries to aim her cannon at the ships, but we are surrounded. She can't fire fast enough. We are the final vessel of our fleet, and the

Empire's cannons are too strong, too many. Our ship shudders.

Alicia is right. We're sinking.

"Abandon ship!" I yell out to her, steering our great vessel away from the Empire's fleet. I know we can't make it, but I want to try to get James and Alicia to safety.

"We won't leave you!" James calls out.

"Never!" Alicia responds, blasting a hole through the side of another enemy craft.

I smile at my brave crew. Always there at my side. Always there, to the bitter end. I change course— straight into the heart of the Empire's navy.

"Then let's give them the fight of the century!" I yell.

Alicia and James cheer. We steady ourselves, prepare for one last hurrah—

And James's watch begins to beep.

"Aww, no," Alicia huffs.

James says, "How is it dinnertime already?"

He stops the alarm on his watch and frowns from atop the derelict fountain. The sculpture is twice as tall as he is, which means it's a great lookout spot for whatever story I'm telling. I stand on the other side of the overgrown gardens, holding an old bicycle tire, while Alicia sits on the balustrade, a piece of plastic pipe on her shoulder.

This abandoned place is ours. No adults for miles around to tell us to stop playing make-believe or yell at us to be careful and not to climb on things. No adults, no rules, which means no limitations to what my friends and I can dream up. In the entire town, this is the one place that actually feels *fun*. At least, for me. James and Alicia don't always feel the same way, but they know we can do whatever we want out here, so they usually agree with any plan I have.

I take the last step out of my story and let my imagination fade into reality. The ships are all gone now, replaced by trees and ruins. The sun sits just above the tree line, casting sharp shadows over the wild backyard.

Over the last few years, the forest has closed in on this old property, like it's claiming back the land. Vines twist over every surface, and trees and saplings poke up from the gardens while birds roost in the enormous fountain in the center of it all.

I can almost imagine how this place once was—owned by some rich mining family, perhaps, the lawns all neatly mowed, the gardens filled with beautiful flowers and apple trees. Everyone walking around in fancy dresses or suits, holding parasols to keep out the hot summer sun. I've dreamed up stories about this place many times, making my friends pretend we are royalty, all money and drama. I have a feeling, though, that my imagination doesn't come close to how amazing this place actually was.

I squint and pretend, the mansion this garden belongs to stretching grandly in front of me, all glittering windows and white columns and flowers dripping from trellises. Then I blink again, and I'm staring at the burned-out husk of a devastated building. Most of the top floor is gone from the fire, though there are parts we can still reach. The once-white walls are charred black and crisped brown, windows gaping and shadowed.

The whole place is full of shadows.

I have no idea who lived there, or what happened. No one seems to know.

No one seems to come here.

Just us.

"What are you having for dinner?" Alicia asks, hopping off the balustrade. She sets her makeshift cannon lovingly beside a patch of dandelions.

"I don't know," James says. "I think my parents are making spaghetti."

"Yum," Alicia replies. "Mine are making tacos."

There's a moment of silence when I don't say anything. They know what that means—my mom is at work again, which means I'll be eating alone. Again.

I wait for them to say, *Hey, Kimberly, do you want to come over for dinner?* They don't. They never have.

It hurt my feelings at first, but I got over it fast. They're still my best and only friends, so I can't really complain when they don't have me over to their houses. It's not like I can really invite them over to mine. I've never heard them invite each other over either.

This summer, we've stuck to the woods.

Here, there's always an adventure to be had.

I set the bicycle tire beside our cannon while James climbs down from the fountain.

"Same time tomorrow?" I ask.

"Definitely," Alicia replies. "Maybe tomorrow we'll blast off into space."

"Or explore a haunted house," I venture. We all look at the abandoned mansion.

The last time we played haunted house, we got so scared that we couldn't return to the mansion for weeks. It didn't help that we disturbed a flock of birds while playing. Their caws sounded like laughing ghosts as they flew off, knocking down statues and ceramics in their kerfuffle.

"Maybe not a haunted house," I say. "We could play castle?"

Again, they look uneasily at the mansion.

"Maybe," Alicia says. "Or we could do a scavenger hunt in the woods!"

"That would be a lot of fun," James chimes in.

I begrudgingly agree.

They're scared of the mansion.

I'm intrigued by it.

The truth is, the only reason they've ever gone near the mansion is because I convinced them to. It was so strange—the first time we walked past, it was like they didn't even see it. I had to get them so close that they were practically walking into the walls. Then they startled, as if I'd blindfolded them and was finally allowing them to open their eyes. It took a lot of convincing to get them to go inside, and even now it's like they forget it exists unless I bring it up.

I don't understand why they're so frightened of it. It's just a burned-down building. The worst thing we've ever seen inside was a dead rat.

And damage. So much damage. But none of it is from vandals—there's no graffiti or broken bottles here. Just nature.

Damage by fire.

Damage from weathering countless storms and scorching summers.

Damage by years of neglect.

Even though it's broken, even though it could be dangerous, I love the mansion. I want to know everything about it.

Who lived here?

When was it destroyed?

What happened to it?

Why isn't the rest of our town so grand?

As Alicia and James start walking away, I think maybe I'll come out again tomorrow on my own if they're too scared. I can pretend to be a princess locked away in her tower, waiting for her knight to come home. Or I can be the brave knight storming the castle, rescuing my waiting prince . . . Yeah, I like that version better. I just need to find a good sword and shield.

I take one last look at the mansion before we tread down the path back to Copper Hollow.

It seems to be smiling at me. The black-window eyes, the crooked stone teeth of the front porch.

As if it knows I will always return.

As if it knows I can't escape its pull.

2

It takes us about fifteen minutes to get back to town.

Copper Hollow isn't huge, but it's not super small either. I don't really know what to compare it to—I've never been anywhere else, except for the places I read about.

We pass by the library, where I get all of my books. It's old like everything else in town, with white walls and large windows that let in just the right amount of sunlight to read by, but not so much that it's too hot in the summer. Right beside that is the police station, though we don't really have crime here, so our one police officer just sits and reads the paper or whatever the librarian, Mr. Jones, brings over for him. There's a grocery store and a post office we don't use anymore because no one gets mail. All of this sits along the main street, the rest of our town spreading out around it in small houses and browned yards with fading picket fences. It doesn't spread very far before hitting the woods and mountains that circle around us, giving our town its name.

I don't live in town. I live on the outskirts, back by the woods. But I'm in town a lot.

There's a new book I want to get, and with Mom not coming home until later, I'm in no rush to get back to our empty trailer.

Sometimes, even my imagination can't compete with the loneliness of that small space.

Saying goodbye to Alicia and James makes me feel even lonelier than when I'm back in the trailer. Because I know the hours between now and when I see them again will stretch on and on.

We pause outside the library.

"Well then, mateys," I say, putting on my best pirate accent. "I'll see yer both tomorrer."

"Aye, aye, Captain," James and Alicia say in unison.

We salute one another, and then the two of them wander back toward their homes while I stand and watch them go, that familiar pang in my chest. Before I can get too emotional—captains don't get emotional—I salute their backs and head into the one place in town that truly feels like home.

The library is old. It feels older than the town itself.

Bookshelves tower above me in the open entryway, reaching far above my head. The ceiling is a faded mural. I think it once depicted our town's history, but it's faded to nothing but blurs of color and faint shapes. Sunlight filters down from the windows, dappling the shelves with orange and yellow.

Mr. Jones is at his usual spot behind the desk facing the entry. He's reading a big leather-bound book with his feet propped up on the desk. He glances over the book at my arrival.

"Hello, Ms. Rice," he says in his papery voice. "How can I help you today?"

I think Mr. Jones may be older than even the library. His hair is wispy and his beard is snow-white, and when he moves his bones creak and snap so loud you can hear it on the other side of the library.

"I'd like to check out my next book," I say. I have to talk a little louder than normal so he can hear, which feels wrong when in a library, but there aren't ever any other people in here to mind the noise.

I have a long list of books I want to read at the library. Mr. Rice keeps them in a stack behind his desk, because no one else comes in to read them and he gets tired from going back and forth between shelves. He often makes me exchange my old books for new ones so I don't leave them around the trailer, but I left my bag at home and he doesn't seem to mind lending me one more.

He shuts his tome and sets it on the desk, then reaches below and pulls out my next read.

"I still think this is too dry for a lady your age," he says.

I shrug. We've had this talk many times. I love reading. Especially books that no one else wants to read. I spend hours browsing through the shelves, picking out the dustiest volumes I can find, no matter their title or subject. I don't always read them, but I like to think that I'm doing the books a favor.

No one likes being forgotten.

Mr. Jones knows what I'm doing. It makes him smile. I don't know if anything else makes him smile.

I don't think he likes Copper Hollow much. But he shows up at the library every day. Like it's his duty, rather than his job. Or like he doesn't know what else to do with his time.

He slides the book over to me and writes my name and the book title down in an old ledger, along with today's date. Then he slides the ledger over to me and I put my initials beside it. In fact, my initials, *K. R.*, fill the entire right column. I guess no one else really *does* come in here.

"Enjoy, little lady," Mr. Jones says.

Mr. Jones is pretty much the only one in this town who helps entertain me, but I do wish he'd stop calling me *little lady*.

I smile anyway and take the book—a history book about our area that's so old it doesn't even have a title embossed on the cover anymore. Mr. Jones is already lost in the pages of his own read as I head out the door.

It's like he and the building have reached an agreement, the same agreement everyone in this town has made with their jobs or their homes:

He stays here, and he does the same thing every day, and he doesn't question what else is out there, or what else he could do. And because of that, nothing bad happens. No crime, no disease, no evil—nothing that I've read about in the books that no one else seems to touch.

I glance at the cover of my book, at the worn fabric and lost name.

No one questions. No one wonders what else is out there.

But I do.

Which makes me think that, maybe, asking questions isn't safe.

Maybe it puts me in danger.

3

Copper Hollow is sleepy in the early dusk light.

Everything looks dusted with orange and rose as the sun sets over the tree line. A few people walk home from work. Otherwise, the streets are pretty empty. No one is out on the park benches or walking their dogs.

They're all at home making dinner with their families. Same as they do every night.

I glance down the street to the diner where Mom works. For a moment, I consider going in and grabbing a booth and reading. It's not like it's going to be busy. I don't know why they keep it open all day when only a few people show up to eat.

Anyway, the thought of going there crosses my mind—maybe Mom will sneak me some French fries and I can sit there and read my book and watch her—but I quickly let it go. I don't know why, but I feel awkward sitting around while she works. Like I should be helping her out. She let me do it once. She even let me keep part of her tips so I could buy a milkshake the next time I went in. Then her boss yelled at her and I was never allowed to help out again.

Some days I think that I'll help her at the diner again when I get old enough.

Most days, however, I think that when I'm old enough, I'm going to leave. Just like my dad did years ago.

"Lost in thought, Kimberly?"

I jump and look over to Mr. Couch, our mayor. He's a smiling old man who doesn't look super official, but he's apparently very important. Currently, he's wearing a faded Hawaiian shirt and cargo shorts. They look as worn out as he does.

"Hello, Mr. Couch," I reply. I give him my widest smile, the one I give every grown-up when I don't really know them. "How are you this evening?"

"I'm doing well, thank you. What have you got there? A new book?"

He gestures for it, and I begrudgingly hold the book out to him. He takes it and flips it over a few times before opening the pages.

"Oh, well, I'll be, this looks like a history book."

"Yeah," I reply. "It's the history of Copper Hollow. I found it in the way back corner of the library."

He makes a *hmmm* noise under his breath and flips through a few pages. Maybe it's my imagination, but his eyes seem to glaze over. He flips a few more pages, then closes the book.

He doesn't hand it back.

He doesn't say anything.

He just stares out at the sunset, still as a statue. The hairs on the back of my neck stand straight up.

"Umm, Mr. Couch," I venture.

He doesn't say anything.

"Hello? Mr. Couch?"

He jolts and shakes his head like he's waking up from a long nap.

"Sorry, Kimberly. Hope you have a nice evening."

And he begins to walk away.

"Mr. Couch!" I yell, polite as I can.

He stops and looks back at me.

"Yes, Kimberly?"

"You still have my book."

His eyebrows furrow for a moment. He looks very confused.

Then he looks down at the book in his hands.

"Oh," he says.

Without another word, he hands the book over to me and walks off, moving as if he's still lost in a dream.

I watch him go.

"What was that all about?" I whisper.

When he's a block away, I turn and head toward my own street.

4

I take the long way home.

Past houses all lit up with families sitting inside for dinner, barely talking to one another. Past the old, abandoned factories that no longer house workers. Past the long, winding road leading toward the mountains that gave our town its copper and its name. I walk the long circle that forms the perimeter of our town, and it takes me all of an hour to do it. By the time I get to the road leading home, I'm tired and using a flashlight to see.

The gravel drive winds its way through the forest

that makes up my kingdom. There aren't any lights to guide the way, but I know this road by heart. Heavy summer heat filters through the trees, carrying with it scents of mulch and leaves and something metallic. The smell always makes me think of coming home.

Not that I really like coming home.

For one thing, we're the only family that lives in a trailer.

It sits on an empty plot of land at the end of the drive, trees stretching up all around it. There are two plastic chairs and a table out front under a tattered awning, as well as an old barbecue pit we sometimes use to make fires and roast s'mores over.

And that's pretty much it.

The trailer itself is painted a pale green that Mom says is called *avocado*, but it has so many rust patches the avocado looks like it's gone moldy. No lights on inside, and for some reason, it looks even smaller tonight, like the forest is pushing in on it.

I shine my flashlight over the trailer and squint my eyes and try to imagine it's something else.

A submarine, readying to go on a top-secret mission to Antarctica.

A green rocket about to be tilted up and launched to Mars.

An elevator car that will descend into mines filled with glowing gemstones.

I want to take the helm and go on a late-night adventure . . . but instead all I really see is my dinky old trailer. Empty. Probably stuffy and hot because we never run the air conditioner.

Home sweet home.

I swallow my disappointment and trudge the rest of the way to the front door. Up the single cinder block step.

The whole trailer sways slightly when I step inside. Sometimes I pretend it's rocking on the sea, especially when Mom gets home late. Tonight, it's just annoying.

I flick on the lights and set my book on the tiny counter, trying not to look around so I don't depress myself. Not that there's much to see—the queen bed at the far end that my mom and I share. The tiny table with two benches where I do my homework and where we sometimes eat together but mostly I eat alone. The shelves and drawers filled with a few books and clothes and a couple of my toys. The small kitchenette—a sink, a hot plate, and a mini fridge. The door leading to our tiny bathroom with its standing shower and sink so close to the toilet you could sit on it while washing your hands and showering off your feet.

I grab a box of spaghetti and plop some into a pot, humming some song from the radio. As my dinner cooks, I flip open the book from the library and scan the first few pages.

I can already tell from the table of contents that it's incredibly dry. I probably won't finish it, but hey, at least I'll have skimmed a book on our history. I'll probably know more than most of the adults—no one ever answers when I ask questions about our town. Our history class covers things like the Civil War and all that, but nothing local. I tried asking the teacher but got a blank stare. And when I tried asking my mom about the mansion in the woods, she looked like I'd started speaking another language. I stopped asking questions about our history a long, long time ago.

Sometimes I wonder if that's the reason my dad left. Or if maybe no one talks about our past because he used to be a part of it.

Something thuds near the bed.

I don't think anything of it. Maybe a falling acorn or a kamikaze squirrel jumping onto our roof. Steam starts rising from the pasta.

Then, like fingers tickling down my spine, a chill washes over me.

It feels like I'm being watched.

My hand slowly makes for one of the butter knives in the sink.

Even though it's probably just a cat outside. Or maybe even Alicia or James playing a joke. I live out in the woods . . . anything could be out there. My imagination explodes with possibilities.

Not one of them is good.

I turn my head

    ever

   so

    slowly.

There, sitting atop my pillow and staring straight at me, is a doll with a terrifying smile and a locket around its neck.

Across its dress, written in dripping black ink, are two words:

BURY ME

Bury me.

The words scream in my head like a curse. My heart hammers so loud in my chest that I don't even think I'd hear myself if I *did* scream. But I don't. I am perfectly silent, too shocked to make a noise; it takes all my effort just to keep standing.

The doll just sits there, wearing a beautiful crimson dress, the single light above my bed casting a spot directly on it. Its head is cocked to the side, just slightly.

It looks like it's been waiting for me.

Deep down inside, I know this is true.

I know this from the way she stares at me.

I don't move, and neither does the doll. Though my fingers *do* shake, and the pasta hisses and steams beside me. I don't turn off the burner. I just stare at the doll.

Her eyes are deep brown and her hair falls past her shoulders in black ringlets. The locket on her necklace is rusted shut with age, hanging heavily from a leather cord. And her dress . . . her crimson dress is more intricate than anything I've ever seen, let alone worn. Who would ruin such a beautiful thing by painting those words? Who would leave it here?

I've never seen this doll before.

I run through the possibilities as my brain clicks into gear.

The door was unlocked. Maybe James snuck the doll in while I was walking.

Maybe Mom left it for me. But that doesn't make sense, because even though she might get me a doll—despite the fact that I'm too old for a doll—she would never, ever get one with *BURY ME* written on it, and I can't imagine she would paint it herself. It's not her handwriting, anyway.

Maybe a burglar came in and—what? Left something rather than stole anything?

No. That doesn't make sense.

That only leaves . . . but no, it's too crazy to think.

There's no way the doll came in here on its own. No way it climbed up onto the bed and sat on the pillow—on *my* pillow, like it knows precisely where I sleep, like it's been watching me.

I tell myself, *There's no way it's been waiting for me.*

I tell myself, *There's no way it's alive.*

I force out a laugh, hoping it will break the tension. If anything, it sounds hollow. It reminds me just how alone I am out here, and how long it will be until my mom comes home.

"Ha-ha," I say. "Very funny. You can come out now, James. You got me."

Silence.

"James?" I say. "Alicia?"

More silence.

The pasta boils over beside me and I yelp, jumping a foot in the air. I turn away from the doll and remove the pot from the burner.

Something moves in the corner of my eye.

I look just in time to watch the doll fall over. It tumbles off the bed and lands on the floor. Upright. Its head tilts to the other side now.

The doll

        is

           moving.

I don't think. I run over and grab it, trying not to notice how cold it is despite the heat in here, or how it stares at me with a wider grin than before.

I get to the door and yank it open.

Then I toss the doll as far into the dark forest as I can.

My door is shut and locked before the doll ever hits the ground.

6

I try to wait up for my mother to come home. For a while, I just sit there, staring at the book I checked out, a baseball bat beside me. When I yawn, I realize an hour has passed and I haven't even flipped past the first page. I don't want to sleep. I don't want to be caught unawares. But another hour passes and there are no noises in the woods—no crunch of leaves as my mom walks home, no creepy giggles of a doll that should not exist. Finally, my adrenaline fades and I think that Mom has to be coming home soon, and she'll ground me if I'm up when she's home so late. I snuggle up in bed and promise myself I'll stay awake.

I'll just pretend to sleep. So she doesn't know.

But she must be working later than usual. Or else I'm just too tired.

I close my eyes. I whisper to no one that I'm not tired.

I can't help it.

I fall asleep.

The first thing I hear in the dream is music.

It drifts through my awareness, a string quartet playing some old-fashioned song I know I've never heard before. But it's familiar. So familiar I find myself humming it as I walk down the wide stairs leading to the dance floor.

My family's friends swirl and curtsy and promenade around me as I move across the glittering marble tile. Candles and lanterns glow brightly on every polished surface, casting a rich, golden light over the crowd. In their fancy dresses and coats and makeup, it is almost otherworldly. Like we are suddenly in the world of fairies. Like I am the Fairy Queen, and these are my loyal subjects.

I like that idea.

I hold on to it as I move across the dance floor, pretending that every bow is a bow to me, pretending that this is a grand ball in my honor, and not for my parents. I spy them on the other side of the ballroom, beside the quartet. They aren't dancing. They are standing there, watching everyone dance, with drinks in their hands and sour expressions on their faces. When my mother catches sight of me, she frowns even more deeply. I wonder what I have done wrong. Is it my dress? She picked it out herself.

Or is it just me? It's always me.

I turn away. Pretend that they aren't my parents, but prisoners, here because of some terrible crime against my Fairy Court, and they must watch everyone dance and be merry while they sulk.

It makes me feel better. A little.

Music swells. The sea of people churns around me. But there is no one here my age to dance with, and although the adults smile at me, no one offers me a dance. I think it is time for me to leave. I have made my appearance, and that is enough to keep my parents happy. Or as happy as they will ever be. I don't think anything I do *really* makes them happy.

I think the only thing that makes them happy is money. But they always want more.

I turn toward the stairwell to return to my room. Only, the stairwell isn't there. I look around, wondering what is happening. I try to press my way through the dancing crowd, but they don't give space. I try to make my way to the exit.

There are no exits.

I push my way through the crowd, ducking under skirts and past moving legs, and reach a wall.

No doors. Just glittering lights and tall, closed windows and a flickering glow outside. Warm, like firelight. How is it light outside, when it's night?

The crowd presses closer. They aren't dancing now. They are watching me. Laughing at me.

Their laughter grows louder and now I see their eyes are glittering.

Glass. Like doll eyes.

No, they *are* doll eyes. And their mouths are painted on, too. Just like the doll I threw out of my bed.

The dancing dolls laugh, and the music swells so loud my ears hurt.

The last thing I hear over their laughter and the cacophonous music is the sound of my own scream.

7

"Kimberly!"

Mom's voice cuts through the nightmare, startling me awake. I nearly tumble off the bed.

My heart hammers in my chest as I try to calm myself down, taking stock of the room. I'm in our home. In bed. Mom is at the kitchen table eating cereal and looking up at me over her book. Sunlight filters through the windows. I'm home. Mom is here. I'm safe.

"Are you okay?" she asks.

I swallow. My heart's still pounding a thousand beats a minute and my breath is hot. But the nightmare is fading fast and so is the fear.

"Yeah," I say after a while. "Just a bad dream."

"Poor thing," she responds. "I'll get you some breakfast."

I flop back on the bed and shut my eyes as I hear her rummage around the cabinets for a bowl. What in the world was I dreaming about? All I remember is glittering golden light. And dancing . . . something to do with dancing . . .

"I have to work in a little bit," Mom says. "Another double, I'm afraid. You'll need to fend for yourself for dinner tonight."

I groan. Not that I wasn't expecting it. She seems to always work doubles in the summer.

"Hopefully I won't be back too late. But could you please pick up your toys tonight?"

Huh?

Something flops on my chest.

"I nearly tripped over this on the front step. I really need to change the entry light."

I open my eyes, dread flooding my veins before I even see what she's tossed my way.

The doll sits on my chest. And she is frowning.

8

"Ew, that's just creepy," James says.

We sit outside our secret fort in the woods. The fort isn't much; its only side is an old wood pallet we found in a ditch, and a ragged tarp stretches above it in case it rains or—as is often the case—it's too hot out and we need shade. The doll lies in the old fire pit we've built in the center, staring up at us angrily.

"You really didn't leave it as a trick?" I ask.

I watch James's and Alicia's expressions carefully,

but neither of them look like they're lying when they shake their heads.

"Pinkie swear?" I ask, just to make sure.

They both hold out their pinkies and shake mine.

That settles it; neither of them left the doll on my pillow. Or set it on my doorstep. Or changed its smile into a frown.

"So . . . who did this?" I ask.

"Maybe Peter?" Alicia responds.

Peter is the biggest bully in our school. He's beefy and mean, but he's not that smart. He'd be more likely to shove a girl than try to scare her with a doll. I can't imagine he'd be this creative.

"No, I don't think so," I say. "He'd think even touching a doll was too girlie. And it doesn't seem like something he'd do, anyway."

"You're probably right," James says. "Do you have any enemies? Maybe spies from overseas?"

"This isn't funny," I say. Though I appreciate him trying to make a joke out of it.

I think about what he asked: Do I have any enemies? Anyone at school or in town who hates me enough to want to scare me? I can't think of any. We've been out of school for over a month and I don't talk to anyone but Alicia and James. And maybe Mr. Jones, but I don't have any late library books so I don't think he'd try to frighten me either.

"I can't think of who would do it," I mutter. "I just wish I knew who was following me around."

"It's a little scary to think that they might be outside your house, watching you," James says.

I hadn't even thought about that part. Now every time I look into the forest, I'll wonder if someone is looking back.

"Yeah," Alicia continues. "Have you told your mom yet?"

"No. I don't want her to worry. She has enough to deal with."

The two of them share a look. Clearly, they think I'm out of my mind for not telling an adult. But if I've learned anything from the adults around here, it's that it's easier to do things yourself and only bring it up to adults if necessary.

So if it isn't a prank . . . what is it?

None of us mention the other option, even though

it's the one thing I've been thinking ever since the doll appeared on my pillow:

What if there isn't someone else involved? What if it's just the doll?

And what if what it wants is me?

It's hard to play make-believe after the doll's appearance.

We try.

We go on a scavenger hunt through the woods, looking for things like rusted paint cans hiding leprechaun gold and broken mirrors that actually reflect another world. But every time we bring something back to our fort, we're reminded of the doll.

Thankfully, it doesn't move.

It just sits there, in its painted crimson dress, frowning at the three of us as if we've broken a grave rule. The air around it seems colder than outside the fort, though I have to tell myself it's just the shade.

Part of me wishes it *would* move. Just as long as it's moving out of my life.

Since it doesn't move, I do. For some reason, I keep getting drawn back to the mansion on my search for items to scavenge. No matter the path I take, I always end up there. Alone.

Without my friends, the place is creepier than normal; I don't want to go inside to search for magical items. It feels like the sky is darker here, and the air colder. I don't like the feeling that the mansion is drawing me in like a whirlpool. At the same time, every time I see the mansion I get a thrill in my chest. Something about it feels like . . . well, it feels more like home than my trailer ever has.

When the sun is high, we reconvene at the fort and go over our favorite finds.

Alicia has found a spatula that will levitate any item it flips, along with some marbles that we're pretty certain will enable us to turn into wolves under the full moon. James has brought back a moldy book filled with ancient spells, but none of us can read them. And I've brought back a window frame from outside the mansion, which I think, if installed in a house, will let ghosts in.

"Why would you want to have that?" James asks.

I shrug. "Maybe we could talk to famous dead people. Like Albert Einstein or Rosa Parks."

"I don't think ghosts like that are attracted to magic portals," James says. "It's usually the bad ones that want to cross over."

We all look to the doll. No one says anything, but the same thought is on all our minds, I'm sure: What if the doll is powered by such an evil ghost?

"You know," Alicia says, "we could just do what it wants."

"Which is?" I ask. Is my best friend suddenly able to read dolls' minds?

She looks me in the eye, completely serious.

"I think that we should bury it."

10

We move quickly to bury the doll.

For a moment, I consider taking the locket from its neck—something about the locket snares my attention, as if it holds something very important. But I don't want to keep anything related to the doll.

I want it gone. All of it.

We walk a little ways into the woods to bury it. James digs into the soft earth with the spatula Alicia found while I clutch the doll gingerly, like I'm holding something plagued.

"What do you think it all means?" Alicia asks.

"I don't know," I tell her. "And I don't want to find out."

"Well, whatever it is," Alicia says, "hopefully doing what it says to do is enough to make this whole thing stop."

I nod. If all I have to do is bury the doll to forget about this whole strange situation, I'll do it.

When James is done, I drop the doll unceremoniously into the hole.

"I feel like we should say something," Alicia says quietly.

"Yeah," I mutter. I stare down at the doll. It stares back up at me; its painted eyes narrow and frown deeper . . . or maybe I'm just imagining that from the shadows. Despite the high afternoon heat, chills race across my skin at the look.

"Get out of my life," I say down to the doll. Then I raise my head and look out to the woods. I don't see anyone through the trees, but I raise my voice anyway. Just in case Peter or someone else is out there, watching and laughing. "And stay out of my life. I'm not afraid of you and this isn't funny, so just stop!"

I realize way too late that even though I'm saying I'm not afraid, I *sound* afraid.

I nod to James, who grimly begins shoveling dirt atop the doll. I watch dirt clump over its evil sneer.

I swear it closes its eyes when the first shovelful hits.

Then the doll is out of sight. Hopefully for good.

When the hole is filled, I stomp the dirt down, and then pile a big rock on top of it. Just in case.

"Okay," I say. I try to make my voice sound happy, but it's hard. Every time I blink, I swear I see the doll staring in the dark behind my eyes. "Let's go on an adventure."

My friends agree. I wipe my dirty hands on my jeans as we head back through the woods to our fort.

I look back to the doll's grave.

Stay away, I whisper in my head.

I really hope the doll will listen.

11

I try to forget about the doll for the rest of the afternoon.

We head back into the woods to climb trees and look for UFOs in the clouds. After an unsuccessful search, we wander through the trails in hopes of finding the lair of a mythical zombicorn. We don't find that either.

But we do find the mansion.

I don't even think we're walking in that direction . . . but I must be wrong. One moment we're tracking down an elusive beast, and the next we're standing at the edge of the expansive grounds. The mansion smiles at me with its broken teeth. Suddenly, the zombicorn is the last thing on my mind.

"What do you say, comrades?" I ask, turning to my friends. "Perhaps it's time we explore the long-lost tombs of the Romanovs?"

"I don't know . . ." James says. He looks up at the sky. We still have plenty of daylight, but I know he's looking for an excuse. He's scared.

"Oh, come on," I say. I grab him by the arm and start dragging him forward. I don't know why I want to get inside so badly. I just do.

"I just hope there aren't any more dolls," I hear Alicia mutter behind us.

I hope she's right.

We wander through the mansion for what feels like hours, searching for the bones of lost kings and queens, or at least clues about where the missing princess may be. By the time we've successfully navigated a few secret passageways, the doll and the burial feel like they didn't really happen. Here, in the dusty, cool catacombs, anything even remotely related to Copper Hollow feels like an illusion.

Until we come crashing back to reality.

We're navigating a passageway I'm sure we've never visited before. The air is heavy and hot around us, and with every step, it seems to grow more oppressive. Both James and Alicia lag behind me. They don't complain, but I know they're growing tired.

I also know they're getting scared.

We've never been this deep in the mansion before. I'm *positive* we are nearing the entrance to a treasure chamber, which means guards, which means either a battle or being very, very sneaky.

I pause outside a door and press my finger to my lips. Stone statues of people with broken limbs tower up on each side. But they don't come alive. Yet. Both Alicia and James freeze, staring up at the statues in wavering fear.

Then I push open the door and walk straight into my nightmare.

It's the ballroom.

Immediately, the games stop along with my heart.

"No way," I whisper.

It's *exactly* like the nightmare. I step inside, awestruck, staring up at the balcony—or what's left of it. Everything in here is charred black and broken by age, sunlight streaming in through the rafters, dripping light over the ruined dance floor. Branches and piles of soot and leaves cover every inch of the place, making it hard to imagine this was once so grand. But I know it was. I can feel it, deep in my gut.

I've been here before.

How could I have dreamed about a place in such detail if I'd never visited it? How could a room covered in ash have transformed into something beautiful in my dreams? I keep spinning around, as though I'm dancing to music I can just barely hear. Something about this place is magical.

Something about it makes me never want to leave.

"We should go," James says from behind me.

I turn with a gasp. I'd honestly forgotten he and Alicia were with me.

"What?" I ask. I'm breathless. How fast was I spinning? "But we just got here."

"I know, but . . ." James trails off. Neither he nor Alicia comes into the room.

"There's so much to explore," I say. "I mean, we've never even seen this place before, and we've been here hundreds of times and—"

"We need to go," James interrupts.

I look at him. Really look. His eyes have taken on a sort of glaze. Like he's not actually seeing the room I'm standing in. In fact, both he and Alicia look like they're seeing a ghost.

"James, what's wrong with—"

"Good night, Kimberly," Alicia says, her voice distant, not quite her own. For some reason, it reminds me of the way Mayor Couch spoke when looking at the history book, or the way the librarian's eyes glazed over when I asked him about Copper Hollow's past. It sounds like she's reciting lines in a play. "We will see you in the morning."

And just like that, the two of them turn and walk away.

I watch them go for a moment, listen to their footsteps echoing down the hall.

"What was that all about?" I ask no one.

A roost of pigeons careens up into the rafters in answer, making me jump and yelp as their feathers fly down around me like snow. When they've vanished into the pink sky above, I look back down to the ballroom. My dream drifts through my mind like ribbons of orchestral music.

I remember walking down that broken stairwell. Dancing numbly through the crowd. I remember the dancers closing in on me. Refusing to let me escape.

And suddenly, my nostrils fill with a scent that I don't think was in my dream.

The smell of burning.

The crackle of fresh fire.

Even though the ballroom is empty, even though there's no sign of a spark or blaze, the scent grows stronger. Heavier. My chest constricts as though someone is pressing up against me and I can't breathe. Can't breathe.

I don't wait any longer.

I turn and run from the ballroom. And I swear it's not just my imagination, not just the wind in my ears or the pigeons returning.

I swear I hear a little girl laughing in the room I've left behind.

12

I run all the way home.

By the time I reach my front yard, I'm panting and covered in sweat. I've also made up my mind: Even though I'm usually entranced by it, I'm not going back into the mansion ever again. I can't get the sound of the girl's laughter out of my ears. I know it was only in my mind. I know I had to have been imagining it. But that doesn't make me any less afraid.

Thankfully, when I get inside my trailer, there isn't a doll waiting for me. Just sticky, congested heat because we left the windows closed.

Not so thankfully, there aren't any leftovers waiting for me either.

I groan when I look in the fridge. A bottle of ketchup. A few cans of soda. A bag of moldy spinach . . . not much to choose from. Looks like it's spaghetti again.

I want to shower, but as I make dinner I realize that it's going to be a while before the trailer cools off. Even after I open all the windows, the hot day doesn't want to leave anytime soon. There's no breeze, and the boiling water on the stove isn't helping matters any.

So, a few minutes later when dinner's ready, I sit outside at our tiny table with a battery lantern and a bowl of pasta and my library book.

It's a little cooler out here, but not much. Crickets and toads chirp in the woods. Clouds slowly skirt across the sky. Moths flicker around my lamp.

I suppose for some people, being alone in the woods like this would be creepy. I've read so many horror books that start out this way. But I can't imagine the sounds of nature ever feeling scary.

That laughter in the mansion, however . . .

"Don't think about it," I whisper to myself. "You're never going back there, and that's final."

I take a bite of pasta and open my book.

A COMPREHENSIVE HISTORY OF COPPER HOLLOW, reads the title page.

I flip past the table of contents, to the chapter titled *FOUNDING*.

It's blank.

"What in the world?"

I skim through the pages. Every single one is the same. Some have chapter headings, like *IMPORTANT FIGURES* and *DATES OF NOTE* . . . but that's it.

Everything else is blank.

Is this some sort of joke?

I reach the back of the book in mere seconds. Why in the world does the library have a blank book on our history?

When I close the cover, I glance down at my bowl. Empty.

Wait, how did I eat all of that so quickly? I barely sat down . . .

Memory blurs. My head swims.

"What are you talking about, Kimberly?" I ask myself. "You've been here for at least an hour."

I think back on what I read—facts and figures about my hometown. I can't remember much about them, but I remember reading them. Just as I remember eating all my dinner. What was I worrying about? That the book was blank?

That's just silly, I tell myself. Books aren't blank. *This one was boring, but it surely wasn't empty. I just can't remember what I read because it was so dull.*

I shake my head. Every time I try to think about what I just read, my memory goes all foggy.

I guess that's what happens when I read an entire history book in one night. Weird.

For a moment, I consider reading it again. Then the idea passes. There are much better books in the library.

The trailer has finally cooled down a bit when I get inside and wash my bowl—Mom hates it when I leave dirty dishes in the sink. A yawn escapes my lips. Wow. I must have been reading longer than I thought. A quick glance at the clock says Mom should be finishing her shift in an hour or so. Time to shower and go to bed. The last thing I need is for her to give me a lecture for being up too late. Even if it *is* summer vacation.

I head to the tiny bathroom and close the folding door. Showers have to be fast, as we don't have much hot water to spare and Mom likes showering when she gets home. I hop under the spray, then turn it off and lather up. I'm just about to turn on the faucet to rinse off when I hear it.

A squeak.

The sound of our front door being opened.

Despite the heat in the shower, chills run down my spine.

"Mom?" I call out. Maybe she's home early?

No answer.

The trailer doesn't move, which makes me feel a little better. If someone were coming in, I'd feel the trailer shake.

Must just be the wind . . .

I turn on the water. Close my eyes and rinse off the shampoo and soap and—

SLAM!

The front door shuts so hard the entire trailer wobbles. I scream and fumble to turn off the water.

"Mom?" I call out louder this time, frantic.

No answer.

No one answers.

I grab my towel and wrap it around myself and look for the only weapon I can find: an electric toothbrush.

Brandishing it like a sword, I slowly, carefully open the door and peek out.

Nothing.

The trailer is empty. It rocks back and forth slowly from the aftershock. Was I just imagining things? No. There's no way; I *felt* that.

I push open the door the rest of the way. I don't let go of the toothbrush.

"Whoever you are," I say, not at all as bravely as I wish, "I know you're out there."

No answer.

I wait.

Silence.

No one at our table.

No one in our bed.

The trailer is empty. No movement. Even the crickets outside have gone quiet.

I heave a sigh of relief and lower the toothbrush. I turn back to the bathroom, to actually brush my teeth.

But first I scream for the second time that night.

The doll is back, covered in dirt and standing in the sink.

She is *not* happy.

13

I don't bother with another burial.

I snatch up the doll and run outside to toss it in the trash can. I slam on the lid and add a few bricks on top. Normally, we use the bricks to keep raccoons out of the trash. Now I'm using them to keep the trash *in*.

"Stay. Away. From me." My words come out in gasps. The blood is pounding so loud in my ears that it takes a moment for me to realize the crickets have started chirping again.

For some reason, that makes me feel a little safer.

I don't risk it, though. As another shiver rushes over me, I run back inside.

I make sure to lock the door behind me.

I'm pretty sure it was locked before.

My thoughts race as I huddle in bed, knees to my chest and covers to my nose, even though it's still way too hot. There's no way the doll could have ended up *in my sink* if someone was carrying it in. I would have seen that, right? If someone had dropped it into the bathroom from the tiny window, I would have seen it when I was getting out of the shower. Or—if they had used the slamming door as a diversion—I would have heard the doll thud into the sink in the silence after.

But that's the only answer my rational mind can think of, and even that barely makes sense.

My *irrational* mind has another idea.

That the doll crept in and slammed the door behind her.

That she ran between my legs when I was distracted and opened the bathroom door.

That she climbed up the sink.

That she had wanted to scare me.

I tell myself that's impossible. Dolls don't move, let alone try to scare someone.

But maybe this one does.

14

It takes a long time for me to fall asleep.

Mom comes home. I keep my eyes squeezed shut. She doesn't ask why the door was locked or why the trash cans are covered in bricks. Maybe she didn't notice. Just as she doesn't notice that I'm awake and trembling.

Soon, she's in bed beside me.

I tell myself I'm safe now.

I tell myself I'm safe, but as sleep draws near, I swear it's heralded by the terrifying sound of muffled giggling.

15

Orchestral music soars around me.

The music soars, but I am stuck.

I am stuck in the middle of the dance floor, spinning madly, trying to escape.

No space in the crowd. They close in, tighter, tighter. I can't breathe. My dress is too tight.

I can't breathe, and when I look up through the swathes of billowing chiffon and satin, when I stare at the dancers' painted faces, I realize they aren't dancers at all.

They are dolls.

They are all fully dolls.

Their limbs are porcelain and their fingers jointed, every movement jerky and sharp. Their large glassy eyes stare off into nothing and their mouths are slashed on their faces in red paint. Some are held up by strings that stretch all the way up to the flickering ceiling. Wait, why is the ceiling flickering? Where is the fire?

The doll dancers close in. Press against me. I need to get out of here. Away from their shoving limbs and terrifying stares. I open my mouth to scream.

That's when I taste the smoke.

As flames curl through the tall windows like encroaching hands, the dancing dolls begin to laugh.

16

"**What do you mean, *it came back*?**"

James sounds unconvinced.

Then again, if he were telling me what I'm telling him, would I believe it?

It's barely nine o'clock. The moment I woke up and saw the trailer was empty, I left. I wasn't going to wait around for the doll to show up. So, grabbing a piece of toast for breakfast, I hustled out of the trailer and jogged to my friends' houses, trying my best not to look at the trash can covered in bricks as I passed. First Alicia, then James. I couldn't be alone that morning. Wouldn't. They seemed shocked to see me so early.

They were even more shocked when I finally told them why.

"Exactly what I said. I was taking a shower and heard the door slam. I went out to investigate. And when I came back, she was standing in the sink."

"No way," James replies.

Alicia hasn't said a thing, but her facial expression says it all:

She believes me, and she is scared.

We walk through their neighborhood, heading toward town because Alicia wants to grab some food for breakfast.

"Where is it now, then?" James asks.

"In the trash," I reply.

"Do you think it will stay there?" Alicia asks quietly.

I look at her. It's the first time she's said aloud what I've been fearing—that the doll is somehow alive. That the doll is, for some reason, after me.

"I hope so," I reply. My words are equally quiet. I

don't like the thought that my friends believe the doll is alive. For some reason, that makes it more real.

"We should go check," Alicia says. "Just to make sure."

I can tell that she doesn't actually want to go through with it. I don't either.

"Is that a good idea?" James asks.

"Definitely not," I reply. I look at Alicia. "Let's do it."

17

We grab some bagels from the grocery store and head straight to my trailer. I try not to bring them here very often. It's not that I'm ashamed of where I live; I'm just super aware of how much better their houses are, and I don't want them to feel sorry for me. Even though there's nothing to feel sorry about.

Although we're on a mission, we don't go straight for the trash can. I can tell we all want to put it off. Instead, we sit at my front table—well, I stand, because I'm being polite—and eat our bagels in silence. Mostly in silence.

James picks up the book I was reading and opens it to the front page.

"This looks . . . interesting," he says.

"Yeah," I reply. I don't look at him. I'm too busy staring at the trash can. Are the bricks in the same spot as last night? "I finished it in one sitting."

"What did you learn?" Alicia asks.

"I . . ."

But I don't remember anything I read. In all the fear of last night, I honestly forgot about the book. For some reason, that really bothers me.

"I didn't learn much," I finally say. "It's about our town's history."

"Sounds boring," James says. He slams the book shut. "Who wants to read about Copper Hollow?"

"Yeah," Alicia says. "It's not like anything interesting ever happened here."

Their voices are both dull, just like yesterday when they left me alone in the mansion. Which makes me think I should probably bring that up. Some other time. First, I have to tackle this.

I make my way over to the trash can. There's no point delaying the inevitable. I can hear my friends flanking me as we crunch across the gravel. My heart hammers in my throat. Slowly, I remove each brick and set them on the ground.

When the last is cleared, I grab the lid. I try to ignore how badly my hand shakes.

And when I remove the lid, I don't know whether to gasp from fear or relief.

The doll isn't there.

18

Panic races through me.

"Are you sure you threw it away?" James asks unhelpfully.

I don't answer. I'm already halfway to my trailer, my mind screaming, *No. No no no.* If someone came by and stole it—or if it *escaped*—this can't be over. I just want it to be over. I want this all to be a bad dream.

I throw open the front door and turn on all the lights.

"I know you're in here!" I yell. To no one.

The trailer is empty.

For a moment, I stand there, breathing heavily, my friends worrying behind me. I don't know what I expected to see. The doll on my pillow again? Or Peter or someone else, sitting at our kitchen table, there to make fun of me? But there's no doll and no bully, and before I can start wondering if I'm losing my mind, I rush in and begin opening cabinets, looking under the table, pulling off the sheets of our unmade bed. I probably *definitely* look like I'm losing it.

"What are you doing?" Alicia asks.

"It has to be here," I say. "It *has* to."

"What if it's not?" James says. "What if it was a bad dream?"

"Yeah," Alicia says. Her voice is quiet, like she's trying to convince herself. "Are you sure this isn't just your wild imagination playing tricks on you? You're always so good at make-believe . . ."

"I *know* it was here last night," I say. I push myself up from where I was rummaging through the lower drawers of our bed and face them. That's when I see the trailer through their eyes. Small. A mess. And me, standing in the middle, looking wild-eyed and frantic. They probably think I'm making it up.

I don't know whether to be angry or to laugh, because if I were in their shoes, I'd think the same thing.

"Come on," I say. "I'll prove it."

Without waiting to make sure they're following, I storm past them and into the woods.

I don't head to the fort. I head straight to the tiny burial mound.

James and Alicia are right behind me, and I make sure they get the chance to see it when I arrive. I expect to find the mound torn apart, maybe scraps of the doll's dress stuck to the twigs. But when we get there, the mound is exactly as it was yesterday—a small, fresh pile of dirt with a few stones on top.

My heart sinks.

No. *I have to be right. Or, at the very least, I have to be sure.*

I drop to my knees and push aside the rocks, then start to dig.

"Kimberly—" Alicia begins. I don't stop or say anything. My hands are coated in dirt and my nails are chipped from the rocks, but I barely feel the cuts and scrapes as I claw through the cold, heavy ground. I barely feel anything except my heartbeat, barely hear anything above my own thoughts of *I have to be right. I have to be right.*

After a few moments of digging, I hit the bottom of the mound.

There is

        no

           doll.

I look up at Alicia. James has already walked away, toward the fort.

"I don't understand," Alicia mutters. I see her mentally sorting things out, trying to figure out how the doll could escape without disturbing the burial mound. And I see her reaching a terrifying conclusion: If the doll could escape from here, then who's to say it couldn't also sneak into my trailer?

I stand.

"Now do you believe me?" I ask.

Alicia opens her mouth, but is interrupted by James's yell.

"Come here, quick!"

Alicia and I exchange a worried glance.

Then we run.

James stands stock-still in front of the fort. It doesn't take long to figure out why.

There, sitting in the middle of our fort, her head tilted to the side, is the doll.

There is something about her that looks a little more human. She's covered in dirt, with twigs in her hair and her cheeks smudged. There's no mistaking it's the same doll, though—from the locket to the scribbled crimson dress, she is pulled straight from my nightmares.

Even worse, written in the dirt at her feet are two words:

NOT FUNNY

"Did you do this?" Alicia asks, looking straight at me. Once more, my heart throbs—but this time, with a note of anger.

"Why would I do something like this?" I ask.

"Because Copper Hollow is boring and you're trying to make it fun with another one of your wild stories?" She doesn't sound accusatory; she sounds like she's running out of options that make sense, and she doesn't like that at all.

I shake my head. Swallow hard.

"This isn't fun."

She doesn't say anything for a long time, just looks at my face. And maybe she can read it in my eyes— the fear, the shock, the frustration—because after a while, she takes a deep breath and looks at the doll.

"What do you think she wants us to do?" Alicia asks. "We already buried her."

And it's then that I know she believes me. Even though I really wish she wouldn't. If she believes me, that means there's something scary going on here.

"I don't think she liked us just throwing her in the ground," James says. "Maybe she wants a real funeral."

"What do you mean?" Alicia asks. "We did what she wanted."

"Maybe not. Maybe this is, like, the doll of a girl who was never properly buried, and she wants a real funeral."

I'm about to say we should take her to the funeral parlor when I realize . . . Copper Hollow doesn't have one. I can't actually remember anyone ever dying. Or being born, for that matter.

The thought is quickly pushed out of my mind.

"We were rude yesterday," James continues. "You have to do it right. Respectful. That's what anyone would want."

Alicia swallows hard. A funeral. For a doll.

It should sound ridiculous, but it feels like a terrible weight settling over the three of us. It raises so many questions, and none of us have a way to find out the answers. I stare at the doll, at her dress, at the words in the sand. There's still a chance this is a sick joke by a bully, but I can't think of anyone in Copper Hollow clever enough to pull it off.

Which means everything James is saying might be real. We might truly be dealing with a possessed doll. I shudder. It was in *my bed*.

"Then I guess we throw her a proper funeral," I say. "Let's just hope it's enough."

The funeral is as grand as we can make it.

Alicia runs home to grab some funeral clothes, and James and I wander through the woods, looking for a place to bury the doll. He suggests burying it next to my pet goldfish in my backyard, since it's close and it might count as a real graveyard.

I don't want the doll anywhere near my house, so I make another suggestion.

An hour later, we are all dressed and arranged at the edge of the old mine. It's blazing hot out even in the shade, and the extra layers of Alicia's mourning wear don't help. She found a couple of loose black dresses and even an old dark coat for James. We fashioned veils for all three of us out of an old black swan ballet tutu. Really, I'd say we've done a pretty good job for an impromptu funeral. Alicia has even brought her kazoo so we can have a burial song.

We stand in a half circle around the tiny pit. Beside us, the road leading to the mine's entrance stretches ominously, barricaded by moldy old boards that couldn't keep out a child. Not that anyone would go down there willingly.

Everyone knows it's haunted. The perfect place for a creepy doll to be buried. Even if this is as close to the mine's entrance as we'll go.

The doll is wrapped in a towel. It's not much of a burial shroud, but it will do. At least, I hope it will do. We also made her a makeshift coffin out of a cardboard shoebox we found in the woods, along with some faded plastic flower petals and sparkly bits of jewelry we had lying around the fort. I hope that if this is real, if she really *does* want a proper funeral, this is enough to satisfy the doll.

And I hope that if this *is* all a prank, it ends here. I can just imagine Peter and his goons in the bushes, giggling to one another as they watch us go through with this. I can see it now: When the doll is buried, they'll come bursting out and make fun of us for being little kids who believe in things like cursed dolls and ghosts.

I ready myself for the humiliation. But at least then it will be over.

"You should say something," Alicia whispers.

"What? Why me?"

"She was on *your* pillow," James says. "Clearly, she's linked to you."

I groan. I know it's true. I just don't like hearing it.

"Fine." I reach down and pick up the bundled doll. "Oh, sweet doll. Your life was too short, and you had many adventures unlived. But it is time for you to be buried. Just . . . please . . . stay that way."

James makes a noise in the back of his throat, and I know it's his way of saying that I should say more. I glance at him and Alicia, then back to the doll. I can just picture her inside the towel, glaring up at me, demanding something better. I don't know why, but something about that mental image makes me think of the mansion, and all my weird dreams.

I guess if I'm going to do this right, I need to actually do it well.

"Okay, okay." I clear my throat and close my eyes and imagine the doll, but this time I see her as a real girl, which just makes my words come out stronger. "I don't know why you came into my life, and I'm sorry that this terrible tragedy fell upon you. It isn't right, and it isn't fair, that your life should be cut so short. I only hope that you are able to find peace at last."

I lean over and gently place the doll into the casket.

"Ashes to ashes, dust to dust," I whisper.

James looks at me and gives an approving nod. Then he leans over and brushes dirt on top of the closed casket. Alicia plays a mournful song on her kazoo.

I close my eyes and ready myself for Peter or whoever pulled this prank to leap from the bushes. Any moment now.

Any moment.

No one shows up. That alone worries me more than I want to admit.

Silence stretches between us when Alicia finishes

playing. A cold wind rustles through the trees, causing the cavern to howl.

Despite the sweat dripping down my skin, I shudder. It sounds like a crying ghost.

"Let's get out of here," I finally say. I turn from the burial mound.

I don't look back.

21

We spend the rest of the day playing.

No matter how hard I use my imagination, however, I can't focus. All I can think of is the doll. Why did it show up? Why would it want me to bury it? Was it a lost spirit needing to be put to rest? Was it a message from beyond the grave? And why do I keep thinking it's somehow related to the mansion and my strange, dancing dreams? Even my "overactive" imagination can't figure out why it suddenly appeared.

I try not to worry about it, but I can't stop. By the time James's watch beeps, letting us know it's time for him to go home, my stomach is in so many knots I can't even think of dinner. Or eating alone in my empty trailer. So I do something I've never done before.

I ask my friends to join me.

"We can drop by Mom's diner," I say hopefully.

They must hear the desperation in my voice. The fear. Because they exchange a look and don't answer right away.

"I don't think I can," James says. "My mom doesn't like me missing dinner." My heart sinks. So much for that.

"I might be able to," Alicia replies. "I gotta run home and tell my parents, but how about I meet you at the diner after?"

I nod, suddenly buoyed. We can have dinner together, and even though my mom works late, I can hang out in the booth and wait for her to be done so we can walk home together. I won't have to worry about running into the doll or anything else scary. Adults make scary things go away. So does being with a good friend.

My friends head to their homes and I make my way to the diner in the setting sun. I pass Mayor Couch along the way. He gives me a wave and walks beside me for a moment; I wonder if he's meeting his wife in the diner for dinner. He's in a different faded Hawaiian shirt. Pink, this time.

"What have you been up to this fine summer day?" he asks. His cheeks are a little red. Sunburned.

Burying a haunted doll, I almost say. I catch myself and instead tell him, "Playing in the woods with my friends."

"Oooh, what was the adventure today?"

I make up a lie that has nothing to do with ghosts or dolls or funerals. Everyone in Copper Hollow knows about my adventures.

"Today we explored the great silver mines of Pluto," I say.

His grin dims.

"I hope you weren't near the old copper mines. They're very dangerous, and we must never go there," he warns.

"Of course not," I fib. I mean, we didn't go *into* the mines. We were far away from the entrance. I try to change the subject. "I finished that book. The one about our history."

"Book?" Mayor Couch asks. "What book?"

"The one I showed you."

He chuckles. "You and your imagination. I don't remember you showing me a book."

I'm about to open my mouth to tell him that he must remember, but we are near the diner and something in his expression tells me not to push it.

Something weird is going on with him. It makes me wonder . . . is it linked to the doll? Or maybe he just has some sort of memory loss?

The tiny bell dings when we step into the diner, and my mom looks up from behind the counter. Her smile widens when she sees Mayor Couch. I'm pretty certain it slips a bit when she sees me beside him.

She definitely looks tired. I know these double shifts drain her, and that's why I try to stay out of her way both here and at home. She comes over and says hello to the mayor, who immediately goes to sit next to his wife. Then she turns to me.

"Hi, honey," she says, distracted. "What are you doing here?"

"Alicia and I are having dinner together," I say, as if it's perfectly normal and not the first time my friend has ever joined me for a meal.

I can tell my mom's worried. Worried that she's going to have to pay for our meals when she doesn't have any money to spare. Worried that her boss will come in and get mad at her. And normally, that would be enough to make me stay at home and eat leftovers or cook ramen. But tonight, there's no way I can go back to the trailer alone.

She's stuck with me.

"Okay, well," she says, "you can have the corner booth. I'll get you both milkshakes." She looks to the mayor, then to me. "Just . . . don't get into trouble, okay?"

I nod.

Little does she know, the reason I'm here is because I'm *already* in trouble. I'm just not sure how much, or if it's finally over.

I wait for a few minutes and watch the diners come in. Mom brings over two milkshakes—both chocolate—and I sip mine and stare out the window at the setting sun and start to worry that maybe Alicia won't show up. Maybe her parents told her she couldn't come, or she got hurt, or the doll found her on the way here. Then I catch sight of her walking down the street. Relief floods through me, and I give her a wave.

She smiles when she steps into the diner and sits down across from me.

"Chocolate—my favorite!" she says, and takes a long sip from her shake. "Sorry I'm late. Mom made me do some chores before letting me leave."

"It's okay," I say. "I'm just really glad you made it."

"Of course," she says. "Why wouldn't I?"

Her response strikes me as odd: I want to say, *Because we've never done this before, because you always have some excuse not to hang out.* But I don't want to push it. She's here now.

Mom comes over a minute later and takes our order. Alicia grins at me and tells me her parents gave her some money, so we order extra fries and another round of milkshakes, and even though I feel a little awkward letting her pay, it feels nice to be having fun with my friend.

We talk about everything—the coming school year, her annoying little brother, the dress her mom is forcing her to learn how to sew. Everything but the doll. It's the one subject neither of us wants to touch, not even in the bright lights of the diner. I can tell that she's thinking the same thing I am: It's over now. And that means we can forget it and move on.

Our town seems very good at forgetting things.

When Mom brings our food, we chow down and spend the time watching the other patrons in the diner. It's kind of strange, watching Mayor Couch and his wife. They don't say anything to each other while they eat. And behind me, I overhear some of Alicia's neighbors talking about the weather.

I mean, that's a normal conversation.

Until I realize they keep repeating the same things over and over again.

I glance over my shoulder at them, but neither of them seems to notice that they're just repeating things as they eat.

"Looks like it's going to be a hot summer," one of them says.

"Yeah, not a lick of rain to be seen."

"Hard times. Hard times."

Then they pause, and a few minutes later, start up again.

"Looks like it's going to be a hot summer."

"Yeah, not a lick of rain to be seen."

"Hard times. Hard times."

I lean forward and whisper to Alicia, "Do you hear that?"

"What?" she asks.

I gesture to her neighbors. "They keep saying the same thing."

I see her furrow her eyebrows and concentrate on what they're saying. The neighbors repeat themselves once more, but Alicia shakes her head.

"No they're not," she says. She giggles. "Stop making stuff up, silly. You had me worried for a moment."

I raise an eyebrow, but I don't question. Because the neighbors are repeating themselves *again*, and if she doesn't notice . . .

I thought it was only the doll, but now that

it's shown up, it's like I'm seeing the truth for the first time:

Something very, very weird is happening in Copper Hollow. And no one but me seems to notice.

22

"Elizabeth!" my mom calls out. Her voice comes from upstairs, and I do my best to stay quiet, to stay calm. If she doesn't hear me, she won't come down here. "Elizabeth, where are you?"

Wait, why is she calling me Elizabeth? Isn't my name Kimberly? The question slides from my mind as the dream falls back into place. No, I'm Elizabeth, and right now I need to hide.

This is my secret cave. This is where Aladdin has hidden the genie's lamp. Where the king has stashed his royal jewels. Down here, I can pretend I am safe.

Safe from their arguing. Safe from the arguments I overheard in the town square.

This is my secret cave, but it is my family's greatest secret as well.

Or at least, it *was*.

Gold glitters from every surface—goblets and masks, candelabras and crowns. Jewels drip down like dewdrops, fat and glistening in the lamplight. All locked away behind iron bars. Locked and safe and secret. Except I found the key. I found the key, and my parents don't know, which means I can hide down here without them ever finding me. I can be as safe as the treasures they've hidden away.

I hear my mother walking away. She will keep looking for me. I'm in trouble. She knows I went into town on my own. She knows I've seen the protests in the street.

She knows I've seen the mines.

I look down to my coal-covered hands.

I've seen the truth, and it has stained me deeper than coal dust.

That's why I'm in trouble.

My mother will never find me down here, and

tonight is the ball for all of their friends. There, I'll be able to blend into the crowd. For a few hours, I'll be able to escape. In the midst of so many people, I will be able to hide from my parents and what they have done to our town.

I will be able to hide.

But not forever.

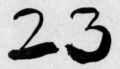

23

"Honey." My mother's voice cuts through the dream. "Honey, wake up."

I grumble and roll over in bed. It feels early. Maybe that's just because I feel like I haven't slept at all. What was I dreaming about? Something about hiding. About being someone else.

At least it didn't have to do with dolls.

"Kimberly Josephine Rice," my mother says sternly.

My eyes snap open.

"What?" I try not to sound as grumpy as I actually am.

"I should ask you the same question."

"Huh?"

She stands over by the kitchen counter, coffee just beginning to percolate. Her hands are on her hips and she stares out the kitchen window, her eyebrows furrowed.

"What is the meaning of this?" she asks. Then she points.

I grumble again and push myself out of bed. I had such a good night—after Alicia went home, I stayed around and read an old magazine until Mom got off of work. She even managed to close up early, so we walked home together, chatting quietly, and there were no dolls and nothing scary and everything finally seemed to be okay again. The funeral had worked.

Something in her tone tells me that relief was short-lived.

I stumble groggily over to her and look out the window. Immediately, despite the heat of the trailer, my blood goes cold.

"Are those your toys?" she asks.

I can only nod silently.

There, in the backyard, are a dozen mounds

popping up from the grass. At first, it looks like there are sticks or something poking out from the tops. Except she's right—those aren't twigs. Those are my old toys. I see a doll's leg and a game board and a telescope, among others.

Someone took my toys and buried them in my backyard!

"Who would—" I begin.

And then I see her.

Sitting on a cinder block near the front of the mounds. Her crimson dress rumpled, her black hair in knots.

A telltale scowl on her porcelain face.

The doll hasn't stayed buried after all.

24

My mom lectures me on "responsibility" and "acting out" and says that I am too old to be doing things like this. Her anger starts turning to sadness, and she says that we are too poor for her to buy me new toys, so I will just have to play with dirty ones. I am grounded for the rest of the day—no playing with James or Alicia—and I need to have the yard back to normal by the time she gets home.

I think her lecture will never end. Then she looks at the clock, curses, and says she's going to be late, and look at how hard she works just so we can get by, yet here I am breaking the toys she's worked for.

I barely hear her. Not as she lectures and not as she runs around the trailer, getting ready to go to the diner for her breakfast shift. All I can hear is the blood pounding in my ears. All I can see is the doll, sitting on her cinder block, staring at me angrily.

I wait for my mother to see the doll. But Mom's either too busy or she doesn't see the same things I do. It's not like I can tell her what's happening. Why would she believe me? My friends barely believe me, and they've seen some of this firsthand.

If this is a prank, it's gone too far. I'm grounded and my mom is worse than angry—she's hurt, thinking that I'd disrespect her like this. I can't stand to think that she's sad, that she's thinking about how little money we have. I spend most of my time trying to prove to her that everything is okay, and now it's clear that it isn't.

The moment she is out the door and down the drive, I stomp out to the backyard and grab the doll.

She is cold. Colder than ice. And I swear that when I pick her up, the air around me goes cold, too.

I want to throw her. I want to toss her into the woods and scream at whoever is out there to stop.

This isn't funny anymore. This was never funny, but now it's *mean*. Someone has come into my house and stolen my toys and gotten me into trouble.

"I don't care who you are or what you want," I growl to the surrounding woods. "I'm done playing games. You hear me? I'm done!"

The woods stay silent. The doll's head tilts to the side. If someone is out there, they aren't interested in coming clean. For some reason, that makes me angrier. A bully like Peter makes sense—I can understand why he'd come around and try to torment me like this. He always does mean things when he's bored, and there's not much else to do around here in the summer.

But if it's not him. If it's the doll . . .

My anger flares.

What right does this doll have, coming into my life and making a mess of things? Why me? Why not someone else?

"If this is your doing," I say to the doll, "I want you to know that I'm done. I buried you. I followed your directions. No more. I want you out of my life. Forever."

The doll doesn't say anything. She just stares at me with a frown that speaks louder than words. I almost want her to respond. To open those painted lips and scream at me, or grab my arm with her tiny hands and try to hurt me. She does nothing. That makes it worse.

This doll is ruining everything, and I can't figure out why, or how to make it stop.

Well, I'm going to end this, once and for all. She might be able to pull herself out of the ground, but she's still made of porcelain and fabric.

I storm inside our trailer, the doll still clutched tight in my fist.

It doesn't take long for me to grab the supplies I need. A book of matches, some newspaper, and kindling from a pile in the back of the yard.

In less than ten minutes, I have a small pyramid of twigs and newspaper built in our fire pit. Normally, this is where Mom and I would roast marshmallows or hot dogs on cool fall evenings. But now, in the morning sunlight, I have an entirely different plan. I'm going to get rid of this doll once and for all. Making sure the bucket of sand for putting out fires is nearby, I light a match and set the twigs alight. It takes a few minutes for the fire to really catch, and I stand back at a safe distance until it is really burning. Then I look at the doll in my hands.

"I'm done playing games," I say again.

Then I toss her into the flames.

She lands right in the middle of the fire. Her dress catches immediately, and the sudden heat makes me take another step back. But I don't leave, even though sweat drips down my face. I'm not leaving until I'm certain she isn't coming back.

"Stay. Away," I say.

I watch her burn.

The paint on her face peels off and the leather cord holding her locket snaps. Her porcelain skin chars black, and right when I think she is finished, when her hair is gone and she is nothing but a shell, her head tilts to the side. Fire reflects in her darkened, glassy eyes. And maybe it's a trick of the light. I don't think so. Because I swear she opens her mouth and silently screams at me.

I don't turn away.

I have to be sure she's gone.

I have to.

I don't step away until she is nothing more than a piece of charcoal. And even then, even when the sun beats down and I am covered in sweat from the fire and the early morning sun, I wait.

I wait until the fire has burned down to embers. Until the doll is ash and the locket is molten.

Then I step forward with the bucket of sand to put out the fire.

As I pour it over the embers, I see that the doll isn't gone. Not entirely.

One tiny arm sticks out from the ashes. Blackened and crisped.

With one finger pointing directly at me.

I shudder. Then I dump the rest of the sand on top.

"There," I say, tossing the bucket to the side. "Now you're *really* buried."

I turn and stomp away.

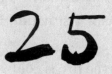

25

I spend the rest of the morning cleaning up the backyard.

I unearth all my toys and clean them off as best I can, keeping a close eye on the pile of sand in the fire pit where the doll found its final resting place. A part of me keeps waiting for the pile to move, for the doll to burst from the ashes like some crazed zombie and attack. Another part waits for someone to leap from the woods and yell at me for burning the doll and ruining their prank.

By the time I've finished clearing up the backyard

and putting everything away, neither of those things has happened, and I've gone from angry to nervous. I know I need to go to the woods and leave a note for James and Alicia—they'll surely be there at noon, our usual time, and I don't want them worrying. Or, worse, coming over here and wondering why the yard is torn up. That's not a situation I'm ready to try to explain.

When I'm sure the fire is cold and the doll is truly gone, I pack up my library book and a pen and paper and head out to the woods.

I must have walked to our fort hundreds of times in the past. I know the path as well as I know the inside of my own trailer—it meanders through the woods, worn down from months and months of my footsteps. Which means I'm not paying attention to where I'm going—my feet already know the way.

Or at least I thought they did.

A few minutes into my walk, I realize the trees are getting thicker. The air is colder. After another few steps, the path opens.

I am standing in front of the burned mansion.

I stop and stare. I swear it's so cold that my breath comes out in clouds.

And it's now, staring up at the ruins, that my dream from last night comes back into focus. My dream where I wasn't myself. I was a girl named Elizabeth, hiding in a room of treasures, yet still pretending I was somewhere else. I know she was hiding in the mansion. I know the two are somehow linked.

"What in the world is going on?" I whisper. As if the mansion will tell me the answers. To my dreams. To the doll. To the strange way everyone has been acting.

The mansion doesn't say a word. Of course it doesn't. For a moment, I consider going inside. Finding my way back to the ballroom. Or seeing if I can find the treasure room . . . if there is a treasure room.

I must be losing it. Thinking my dreams are real. If there were a treasure that huge in Copper Hollow, the town wouldn't be as poor as it is.

I sigh. I need to get to the fort. It's nearly noon, and James and Alicia will be waiting.

I'm about to turn away when I catch it. The slightest hint of movement in one of the broken windows. A splash of crimson darting into the shadows. My chest constricts and ice pools in my veins.

No.

It has to be a bird. A cardinal.

But I swear it was the doll.

26

I don't think—

I run.

Away from the mansion and its toothy grin, deep into the woods that have always—up until right now—felt like home. Despite the heat of the day and the sweat from running, my skin feels cold as ice. Even the scent of the forest is different—where it once smelled like lush green heat, it now smells cold. Dusty. Like a graveyard.

But that's not the worst part.

Drifting through the trees is the giggling of a little

girl. Familiar and haunting enough to send more chills down my spine.

Something darts through the underbrush.

I jerk around. Was that another cardinal? That flash of red?

More giggling. I turn and something darts through the branches above me, fast as I blink.

No, it can't be a doll. It has to be a bird. Has to be.

I have to get out of here.

I try to ignore the phantom doll and the giggling and the cold. I run full speed through the woods, toward our fort, and pray that the nightmare stays behind me.

By the time I get to the fort, it's way past our normal meeting time, and I have mostly convinced myself that I was just seeing things in the woods, because the closer I got to the fort, the less, well, spooky the woods became.

But James and Alicia aren't there.

Strange. Maybe they were already here and just left without me. The thought leaves a pang in my gut—I don't like thinking they're out having fun when I'm grounded. Not that I want them to be miserable without me. I just . . . don't want to be alone.

At least the air is a normal temperature here, and there aren't any more signs of a doll. The panic in my chest starts to go away, but I still jolt every time I hear the branches rustle from a squirrel.

I leave my friends a note, just in case they head back this way:

> Got in trouble. Can't play today. Hopefully tomorrow.

I don't want to mention being grounded because of the buried toys. I don't want to admit the doll came back. That I burned her, but now I think she's following me. That's beyond impossible, and I don't want them to worry over nothing.

I tell myself I was seeing things before, that it was just stress and nerves and fear of stumbling upon the mansion alone.

The doll is nothing but a pile of ash now.

She has to be.

There's no point frightening Alicia and James when everything is taken care of.

I make my way slowly back into town, keeping my

ears peeled for sounds of my friends' laughter. Even though my mom told me I'm not supposed to play with them, she wouldn't know if I *accidentally* ran across them and *accidentally* started to join in their games.

If I'm being perfectly honest with myself, I'm also on high alert because I expect the doll to return at any moment.

"She's just ash now," I keep whispering to myself. "She's gone. It's over."

It's over.

So why don't I feel like that's actually true?

A few minutes later, I make it to town without sight of the doll or my friends. But I do catch sight of the one person I don't want to meet.

Peter.

I'm on the front steps of the library, and I consider making a run for cover inside. But too late. The second after I see him, he catches sight of me.

Do I run? Hide?

No.

I don't want to be bullied anymore. The tricks with the doll have gone far enough. I clench my fists as he stomps his way over to me. I'm not going to run. I'm going to stand up for myself.

I've already destroyed the doll. Now I'm going to tell him to stay away from me.

"What are you doing without your dweeb friends?" Peter asks.

He's only a year older than me, but he's a lot bigger—his dad has a farm on the edge of town, and Peter clearly spends his summer days helping out. His shoulders are sunburned and his arms are the size of my neck and his face is meaner than a cornered cat. Normally, I'd flinch. He's never hit me before, but that hasn't stopped him from making my life miserable with his mean comments or tricks. I'm not backing down now, though.

"I'm not playing with them today," I say. I try to keep my voice firm, but it shakes a little. It's hard to sound mean and strong when you're staring up at someone. "I'm grounded. Because of you."

Peter snorts.

"Because of me?"

"Yeah," I say. I take a step forward. "I don't know

why you're picking on me, but you need to stop. I destroyed the doll and I don't want to see it ever again."

Peter's eyebrows furrow in confusion.

"Doll? I don't play with no dolls."

"The one you've been torturing me with," I say. "Real clever. Sneaking around my house and trying to freak me out. Well, it's over now, so you can just stop."

My words aren't as confident as I want them to be, and the more I talk, the less sense I'm making. Especially since Peter just seems to get more and more confused.

"I haven't been near your house," he says. "I don't know what you're talking about. And I've never touched a doll in my life."

"Is there a problem here, children?"

I jolt and turn around.

Mr. Jones stands in the doorway of the library, looking at both of us very solemnly. Particularly at Peter.

"Nothing's wrong," Peter says. He glares back at me. "Kimberly is just making stuff up."

Before I can say anything to defend myself, he turns around and stomps off. I watch him go, then shakily make my way up the final steps to Mr. Jones.

"Is he bothering you?" Mr. Jones asks.

I swallow hard. I was so certain that Peter was the one behind the doll, but . . . although Peter is many things, a good liar isn't one of them. He looked truly confused, and truly angry that I'd accuse him of having a doll. Even if it was a doll meant to make my life miserable.

But if he's not behind it . . .

"I don't know anymore," I say.

27

Mr. Jones opens the door for me, and I follow him inside to drop my book off. The dusty old tome sits on top of the library desk while he roots around for my next read. He pulls it out from behind the desk and sets it beside my old book. This one is on the geology of Central Colorado, which I doubt I'll read at all. Then again, I don't really have anything else to do today.

"What did you learn from this one?" Mr. Jones asks, tapping the cover of the history book.

"I don't really remember," I admit. "It's kind of a blur."

Mr. Jones smiles. "When you get older, that's all history becomes—a big blur."

I smile weakly in return. Mr. Jones seems to know more about this place than anyone else, but he's never been quick to offer information. Maybe, since we're on the subject . . .

"What do you know about the mansion in the woods?" I ask.

"The mansion in the . . ." His words trail off as if he's drifting into thought. I honestly expect him to tell me not to ask questions about it, or to pretend he doesn't know anything about it like everyone else in town. Instead, after a few moments of silence, he answers.

"It's a dangerous place," he says. "A great tragedy happened there, many, many years ago. A fire, if I recall. Yes, a fire. Such a shame."

"But who lived there?"

Again, the hesitation before answering.

"A family," he says. "A husband and wife. And their young daughter. They ran the mines of Copper Hollow, way back when the mines were open."

"What happened to them? Are they still here?"

Mr. Jones opens his mouth, but no words come out. He blinks a few times. Swallows.

"I'm sorry, young lady," he says. "What were we talking about? Old age, you know."

I groan under my breath, but I know not to press it. His eyes have taken on the same glazed look as when Mayor Couch saw the book the other night.

No one wants to talk about the mansion or the family who lived there. But at least now I know there *was* a family. And that they had a daughter. It's more than I've ever learned before.

"Don't worry about it, Mr. Jones," I say. I grab the new book. "Have a good afternoon."

I don't head home.

I sit outside the library for a long while, watching my sleepy town pass by. A few people walk their dogs while others go for a jog. Mostly, though, the wide boulevard of our downtown is empty, filled with hot golden sunlight and dust. Once more, my dream filters through my head—the room filled with riches, the girl hiding from . . . something. It felt so real, and even now, in the light of day, it seems more like a memory than a dream. But none of it fits with the reality of Copper Hollow. There are no fancy parties here, no rich families. At least, not anymore. There's just endless days of nothing new. My imagination is just trying to make this place more interesting than it is. More interesting than it will ever be.

For some reason, that makes me think of my dad.

He's the only person who's ever left this town, at least to my knowledge. My mom says he left a few weeks before I was born, that he promised he would find a better life for us. Somewhere far away from here.

Maybe he found it. He probably did—it wouldn't take much.

The trouble was, whatever he found was so good he didn't want to come back. He left us here, in a town with nothing going on. He left my mom and me in a trailer, where no matter how hard we work, we never get ahead.

"Get ahold of yourself," I mutter. There's no use dwelling on the past. He left us. That's that.

I haven't thought of my dad in years. Haven't even really thought about actually leaving here, though

I wonder now if maybe someday I'll go find him. Wherever he is. Find him and ask him why he left us here, and what is so much better outside that makes leaving his own family worth it.

It must be the stress of the doll making me think such things. Yeah. It must be that.

Even though the thought of him leaving makes me sad on one hand, on the other, it fills me with a sort of fire. I want to follow in his footsteps. I'm going to take my mom and my friends and we are going to leave this quiet little town once and for all. Move to a city. Have a real life. A life worth living.

Like my dad, I won't come back here.

Unlike him, I won't leave the important people behind.

Steeling my resolve, I push myself to standing and stare down the one road leading out of town, the one that cuts past the copper mine and out into the unknown beyond.

"Someday soon," I whisper to myself.

I'm going to get out of this town and its creepy dolls and its strange happenings.

I'm going to escape. And nothing is going to stop me.

It's late.

It's quiet.

Too quiet.

The crickets have stopped chirping and my mother has stopped snoring. When I roll over in bed, she isn't there.

That is my first clue that something is wrong. Terribly wrong.

"Help me," a voice says. I turn back.

The trailer disappears, replaced by a room filled with gold and jewels. Gold and jewels and smoke, and a girl standing in the corner in a beautiful crimson dress. The same dress as the doll.

"Help you?" I ask. I cough.

Smoke creeps thicker. And above us, far away, or maybe not far at all, I hear the crackle and roar of fire.

"Bury me," the girl says.

I blink, and she is the doll. The doll, but my size. They have the same fancy red dress, the same curly black hair. The same angry smile on her face. And as smoke thickens around us and chokes my nostrils, she smiles. Her dark doll eyes glint with firelight as she takes a step forward. Another step, and she is right in front of me, her cold porcelain hands on my neck.

"Bury me," she says, "or I'll bury *you*."

I wake up with a scream.

Sunlight pours in through the windows. It illuminates the empty trailer, the folded newspaper on the table, the half-full carafe of coffee on the kitchen counter. Mom must have already left for work. Immediately, my nightmare fades. It was all just a dream. I'm safe.

I flop back down on the bed with a huge sigh and close my eyes. It feels like I haven't slept in weeks.

THUD

Something slams atop the trailer roof. My eyes snap open. An acorn? A squirrel? That would have to be an awfully big—

THUD

It comes again. But on a different spot.

THUD

    THUD

      THUD

I jolt upright and clutch the covers to my chest as the trailer fills with the sound.

Not just thuds—

Footsteps.

Dozens of tiny footsteps, scampering across the trailer roof. And with them, the sound of high-pitched laughter.

The sound builds and builds until I swear my ears are going to explode. I duck beneath the blankets, pull them over my head, and squeeze my hands to my ears.

This can't be real. *This can't be real.*

Then, as if cut off with a knife, the footsteps and laughter stop.

Just the quiet.

The pulse of my frantic heartbeat. Then—

KNOCK KNOCK KNOCK

A pounding at the front door. I swallow and cower under the sheets. I don't move. I barely breathe. No other sound enters the trailer.

And for a long time, I lie there, listening to the quiet and my heartbeat, trying to force my pulse to slow, until I start wondering if I'm making it all up. Maybe it's another dream—I've had them before, when you think you're awake but you're still asleep. It has to be. There's no other option. There's no way my trailer is being overrun by dolls. No way one of them has knocked at the door.

The doll is gone.

She has to be gone.

After what feels like an hour, I pull back the sheets and look around.

There's still the folded newspaper on the kitchen table. The half carafe of coffee. The morning light.

Shakily, I get out of bed.

"It was all just a bad dream," I say to myself.

Birds sing outside the trailer. It's daytime. I'm awake.

I pinch myself, just to make sure.

It stings. Definitely awake.

I make my way toward the door. I'm awake, and

everything that just happened was a bad dream.

I'm going to prove it to myself.

My fingers shake on the doorknob. I take a deep breath. Tell myself once more that this is silly. I have nothing to be scared of. It's morning. The doll is ash. Everything was just a bad dream.

Before I can psych myself out more, I yank open the door.

And there, on the front stoop, is the doll.

Written in soot across the step are the same two words as on her dress, in the exact same creepy handwriting.

BURY ME

I slam the door shut. And the moment I do, the knocking starts again.

Knock
    Knock
        Knock
  Knock
    Knock
        Knock

At first it's just the door.

But then it's also the walls.

All the walls.

KNOCK

    KNOCK

        KNOCK

And the roof.

THUD

    THUD

        THUD

This isn't possible.

It isn't happening.

But it IS happening.

Our trailer has never seemed so flimsy. The walls are going to cave in.

I am trapped.

And there's so much noise.

A hurricane would be quieter.

A tornado would be less terrifying.

How is one doll doing this? Unless . . . there can't be more than one doll. Can there?

I don't know what to do.

I curl up on my bed, rocking back and forth and staring at the locked door.

We don't have a phone, so I can't call my mom to help me. I can't reach out to Alicia or James. I'm stuck in here, with a possessed doll outside my front door, and there's nowhere to go and nothing to do. I'm not even safe in here.

The windows could break at any moment.

The walls could fall at any moment.

The ceiling could crash.

What have I done to deserve this?

Why won't she stop?

What if she never goes away?

The thought is enough to make tears come to my eyes.

"Stop it!" I yell out. "Please, just stop!"

And all at once, it stops.

Silence.

And then. Rather than a thousand individual knocks, the whole trailer shakes, as if one giant hand is reaching everywhere at once.

Knock. Knock. Knock.

Knock. Knock. **KNOCK.**

I can't stand the thought that I'm going to have to deal with this forever. And for some reason, that's enough to make me stop being scared, just for a moment. I refuse to be bullied by a doll. By now, I'm positive this isn't someone playing a prank. This is real. And that means I really have to find a way to stop it, before it takes over my life any more than it already has.

"You can do this, Kimberly," I say to myself. "This is just a stupid, tiny doll. You can handle this."

I think of the many different expeditions my friends and I've gone on: trips to the Arctic to study mechanical polar bears, expeditions to Mars and space races across Saturn, escaping haunted houses filled with scary ghosts and zombies.

We've always managed to get out.

I need my friends to help me.

Emboldened, I get dressed and grab my backpack. As I do

the knocking

falls

silent

as if the sound itself is waiting

for my next move.

I'm not certain what I'm going to do, but I *am* certain that my friends will be able to help. Together, we'll come up with a solution. I'm sure of it.

We don't have any other choice.

I slam open the door, expecting to see a horde of dolls. Or maybe one giant doll.

But there, sitting on the step, is the exact same doll as all the other times.

The one I buried.

The one I burned.

Only there's no sign of dirt or ash; her dress is perfect crimson, her skin pure porcelain, her hair perfectly combed. The locket still sits heavily on her neck, and the words *BURY ME* are still scrawled on her dress. But her face is different. The frown has deepened, and I can see tiny teeth peeking out between her red lips.

THAT WASN'T NICE is written in the dirt at her feet.

I swallow and look around.

No one else in the yard. Just a clear summer day. Birds singing. Insects chirping. As if everything agrees that nothing could be going wrong. Tears form at the corners of my eyes.

Why won't she go away?

"What are you?" I ask, my voice cracking.

Then, before she or anyone else can answer, I rush forward and shove her into my backpack, jogging down the path to town without a single glance back.

36

"Are you *sure* it's the same doll?" Alicia asks me.

I nod solemnly. She's always been the analytical one. Which is good, because James's imagination and my imagination can often become overpowering when we're all together.

We're back in our fort, and the doll sits between us. Just as it did a few days ago. Only now, the air between all of us feels different. Charged and heavy, like a thunderstorm just about to break.

I'm worried to find out what happens when it does.

"And you're sure it's not a prank?" James says.

"How could it be a prank?" I ask. "We buried her, and she came back. Then I threw her in a fire and watched her burn—but now she's back. I even confronted Peter about it yesterday, and he had no clue what I was talking about."

I haven't told them about the knocking on the trailer. For some reason, admitting that seems like a big mistake. They're already worried. If they think I'm actually in danger—if I *admit* that I might be in physical danger—I don't know what they'd do. We just have to solve how to get rid of the doll, and then I know that everything else will go back to normal.

Alicia bites her lip. She kneels before the doll and pokes it. The doll tips over; I fight back a yelp.

"He could have been lying. And there's a chance there could be multiple copies of the same doll," she says. She looks around and drops her voice. "We have to make sure the same one is coming back."

"How?" I ask.

She just smiles grimly and turns her attention to the doll. She lifts up the hem of its dress, pulls out a small marker, and writes ☺, the number *42*, and the letters *ZXR* on its leg. When she flips the dress back and stands up, I can't tell she's made a mark.

"What does that mean?" James asks.

"Nothing," she replies. "It's nonsense. And no one but us saw what it was." Again, she glances around the woods. We all look, but there's no way anyone could be hiding out there. At least, not close enough to see the tiny letters.

"Now what?" James asks.

"Now we test Kimberly's theory," Alicia says. "We see if the doll truly is coming back from the dead."

We burn the doll a second time that afternoon.

No funeral. No speeches. Just a fire in the pit behind my house.

We all watch it burn in silence.

I swear, over the hiss and the pop of burning wood and cracking porcelain, I hear something. Faint as the wind rustling through the leaves. Screams. Distant screams, someone crying far away.

I glance toward the woods and swear the sound is coming from the mansion.

"What's up?" Alicia asks.

"Do you hear that?" I ask.

James and Alicia look at each other. That's answer enough for me.

"Never mind," I say.

I try to drown out the sound and the building ache in my chest—the fear that this won't work. The fear that something terrible will happen as a result. Alicia keeps looking at me worriedly. She doesn't ask anything. I don't think she really wants to know the answer.

We don't move until all that's left of the doll is ashes. And when the ashes are cooled, we each scoop a handful into separate tins and bury the rest. For extra measure, Alicia secures the lid on each tin with duct tape.

"We don't let these out of our sight," Alicia says solemnly. "Sleep with it on your nightstand or under your pillow. If the doll is coming back from the dead, there's no way it will be able to return without its ashes." Then her serious expression breaks and she smiles at me. "See? Problem solved. You won't be haunted by a creepy doll any longer."

"But what if it *does* come back?" James asks. He holds his tin gingerly, like he doesn't want it anywhere near him. I know the feeling. If I could have Alicia watch my tin without feeling like a coward, I would.

"Then we go to the police."

I hold back a snort. The only policeman in this town is Officer Frank, and I think he spends more time napping than he does actually policing.

Even quieter, James asks again, "But what if it still manages to come back?"

My heart sinks with his question. Because I've been thinking it, too.

"I don't know," Alicia admits. She looks at me. "We just better hope that doesn't happen."

Even though I'm no longer grounded, playing with James and Alicia isn't nearly as fun as it should be. Mostly because none of us want to be alone, which means our usual games of scavenger hunts or hide-and-seek are off the menu. It's too hot to leave the cover of the woods or the fort, or to do anything really fun like climb trees. If only there was a lake nearby we could visit, or a swimming pool. Instead, there's just the heat and the bugs and the forest.

And the looming presence of the doll's cremated remains.

"Maybe we could go on a quest?" Alicia ventures. "The fort can be a submarine and we're heading down to the bottom of the ocean to look for sunken treasure?"

James and I agree to take part, but after a few minutes of trying to get the story rolling, we give up. It's too hot to pretend we're underwater. And besides, we all keep looking at the taped tins we have stacked beside the fort. We're watching to see if they move, or break open, or disappear.

The doll is gone, but she's all we can think about.

After a while, we each grab our tins and head home. It's still a few hours before dinner, but the mood between us is heavy. Expectant. We can't concentrate on having fun when we're worried about what will happen next.

At least, for the first time, it seems I'm not alone in that fear.

I trudge back home. Even though it's still incredibly hot, the tin box feels cold in my hands, like it's holding ice. A small part of me wants to open it and see if the ashes are still inside, or if they're starting to re-form into a doll leg or something, like a caterpillar metamorphosing in its cocoon. The rest of me doesn't want to see the truth. I don't know what I'd do if the doll *was* whole inside there, beyond scream and run to the town's exit as fast as I can.

I'm so caught up in thinking about the doll that I don't even realize the trailer isn't empty until my mom clears her throat.

"I didn't expect you to be home already," she says.

She's sitting at the front table, a glass of lemonade in one hand and a book on her lap. Strange.

"What are you doing home early?" I ask. I thought she was working another double. She seems to *always* be working doubles lately.

I try to smoothly hide the box behind my back, but of course she notices.

"What's that?" she asks.

"Scavenger hunt," I reply quickly. I walk over and sit on the chair beside her. "You didn't say why you're home early."

She sighs. "Fridge went out in the diner, so they sent me home."

"Yay?"

"I guess. It means no money tonight."

I don't say anything to that. Just yesterday she was yelling at me because she thought I'd ruined my toys to disrespect her. I can tell she's still thinking about it.

"So what did you find in the hunt?" she asks. She nods to the box in my lap.

I swallow.

"What do you know about the mansion in the woods?" I ask.

I don't really know where the words come from. She doesn't usually care where my friends and I play or what I do, so long as I stay out of the mines and don't get into trouble.

I'm watching her eyes when I ask. I want to see if she's going to go blank like Mayor Couch or the librarian. But her forehead furrows like she's thinking hard.

"The mansion in the woods . . ."

She trails off. Is that the end?

Then she looks at me and her face is serious. Angry.

"Nothing good has ever come from that mansion," she growls. "You must stay away from there. Just like your father—"

Her eyes unfocus. *No, no!*

"What about Dad?" I ask. "I thought you said he left town and never came back?"

She raises a hand to her forehead as if checking her temperature.

"What?" she murmurs. "What were we talking about?"

"Dad," I say. "Dad and the mansion and—"

"Your father left us," she says, monotone. "And there is no mansion."

"But I saw—"

She winces at my voice. I didn't realize I was yelling.

"You and your imagination," she says. "Ugh, this heat. I suddenly have a migraine. I'm going to go lie down."

I watch her go. I watch the trailer shake as she makes her way to the bed and am suddenly reminded of the horrible noises from this morning, the thuds and knocks that nearly crumpled the trailer in on itself. A part of me wants to yell out, to warn her. The rest of me knows . . .

I glance at the cold box in my lap.

The rest of me knows that the doll isn't after my mom. She's after me.

And hopefully, now, she can't get either of us.

32

"Elizabeth!" my mom calls out.

My dream memory shifts. Elizabeth? But my name isn't Elizabeth, it's . . .

"Elizabeth, you come out right now or you are grounded, you hear me?"

I hear the rumble of another voice. My father.

"I can't find her—she's been hiding all afternoon," my mother growls loudly. "I just can't bear this right now. I have to get ready for tonight."

Another baritone rumble as my father responds, then the distant thud of my mother's departing footsteps.

I close my eyes against the darkness.

They won't find me no matter how hard they look. I know, because I only just discovered the treasury this week—the stairway hidden behind a grand portrait of my grandparents, and the room itself locked by a key I found nestled in my father's desk. Now I hide behind another portrait, one of my father and uncle. In the portrait, they look happy standing together. I have never seen them that happy in real life.

I haven't seen my uncle for years, until today.

"Elizabeth," my dad says.

I jolt—I've been so focused on pretending I wasn't there, I haven't heard him come into the treasury. I hold my breath and don't make a sound.

"Elizabeth, I know you're in here," he says, then sighs. "I also know you went into town today, and I hate to think of what you might have seen. Or what it might have made you think of me."

I close my eyes once more and pretend I'm not hearing this. But this is the one thing I can't pretend away.

My father is a monster.

That's what everyone in town thinks. Especially

the miners. After what happened last week, when part of the mine collapsed and he forced them to continue working, even though it was dangerous . . . It's no wonder the miners are refusing to work. No wonder they are protesting in the streets. They all think my parents are after only one thing: money. No matter the cost. No matter the risk.

The worst part is, I know they are right.

My parents will do anything for money. My parents don't care about human life. Not even mine.

"I brought you a gift," he says. "I'll leave it right here. I do hope you decide to come out. The ball tonight will be a spectacle, and it would mean the world to your mother and me if you chose to attend."

If you chose. I have no choice—if I don't appear at the ball, I will be worse than grounded. They don't care about me going, they don't care about me having a good time. They only want me to be on display. Their perfect little daughter. The admiration of all of their rich, disgusting guests.

The only thing my parents like more than money is admiration.

"Okay, well, I must go get ready, my dearest. And

hopefully you will as well. I have no doubt you will look stunning in your new dress."

There's a rustle and the clank of the iron-bar door shutting behind him. He doesn't relock it.

I count to one hundred. When I'm positive he is no longer around and my hiding spot won't be given away, I step out from behind the painting.

Despite the fear and the anger battling in my chest, the sight of what he's brought me makes me gasp with happiness.

He has brought me a doll, and she looks just like me.

33

I wake up in the middle of the night with a jolt.

My mother sleeps soundly beside me, and the trailer is dark, lit only by a slash of light from the white floodlight outside. My heart is racing and I desperately try to hold on to my dream. I know it's important.

In the dream, I was a girl named Elizabeth.

In my dream, I was hiding, because my parents were upset that I'd gone into town on my own and seen . . . something. Something that would make me think my parents were monsters.

Something to do with the copper mine.

And then my father gave me a doll. No, not *a* doll, *the* doll. The same hair and dress, the same creepy eyes and smile.

In the dream, it had filled me with joy.

Now it only fills me with fear.

What in the world is going on? Am I reliving someone else's past? I know that my dreams the last few nights have been related—I can't be making this stuff up. Not even *my* imagination is enough to create something like this.

So who is Elizabeth? And why am I being haunted by her doll?

Instantly, I look to the tiny nightstand. As quietly as I can, I crawl over Mom and slide open the drawer. When I see the duct-tape-wrapped tin still inside, I let out a huge sigh of relief. The ashes are still here. I'm still safe.

I slide the drawer shut and make my way back to my side of the bed.

In the morning, I'll check the library again to see if I can find anything out about Elizabeth and the family who lived in the manor. If nothing else, I'll learn if what I'm dreaming is fact or fiction.

At least I don't have to worry about the doll.

I slide under the covers.

My foot bumps something at the bottom of the bed.

My skin goes cold immediately.

Quietly, shaking, I double over and reach down toward the bottom of the bed.

My fingers wrap around the cold body of a doll.

I swear my heart stops
  as I pull the doll out
  as I hold it up in the slash of light
  as I see the same face,
        same dress,
        same *BURY ME*
  as I flip up the fabric
  as I examine the marking on its leg:
          ☺. 42. ZXR.

"No," I gasp.

It's the same doll.

Somehow, even though her ashes have been divided and sealed up, she's come back.

34

I don't sleep for the rest of the night.

I try to find someplace to seal the doll away.

I put her in the nightstand. But as soon as I close the drawer, I swear I hear her moving inside. I glance at my mom, but she sleeps through the noise as if it isn't happening.

I throw the doll in the refrigerator and push a chair against it. I hear her clawing and scraping on the inside, then breaking all the eggs and pouring out the milk so it leaks from the door when I open it again. Once more I look to my mother, but she doesn't wake. I snarl at the doll—who doesn't move at all when I can see her—and grab a towel. With the doll in one hand and the towel in the other, I mop up the milk and the eggs.

I consider waking my mom. Making her deal with this. But I have a feeling that the doll won't do a thing under my mother's gaze. All it will do is get me in trouble—Mom needs her sleep so she can get to her opening shift, and if I wake her up yelling about a live doll that only moves when out of sight, she will ground me again for my overactive imagination. I'm so frustrated as I mop up the milk.

I just. Want. This. To. Stop.

Finally, when the mess is mostly clean, I wrap the doll in my pillowcase and put her under my body. I don't expect to sleep, but at least she can't get into trouble with me smothering her.

I can feel her pressing against me the whole time, her cold, tiny fingers digging into my back, her painted lips wordlessly mouthing my name.

I hear the pillowcase rip. I turn over and grab the doll, holding her tight to my chest. I won't let her escape. I won't let her get me into trouble.

I keep my eyes open the entire night, staring at

my mother sleeping peacefully, tears rolling down my cheeks. The doll won't stop.

She will not be ignored.

The next morning, as soon as I can, I run all the way to Alicia's house.

"What's the matter?" she asks blearily when she answers the door.

I know I look a mess; after the doll came out of the pillowcase, I couldn't let her out of my sight. I stayed up until the sun rose, clutching the doll tight, refusing to shut my eyes for fear she would escape—or do something evil to me and my mother as we slept. But then, when my mother finally woke up, she didn't mention hearing anything in the night, not the breaking eggs or rumbling nightstand, and I did such a good job cleaning everything up I can't see any mess.

It makes me wonder if I dreamed the whole thing.

The only proof is the doll I still hold in one hand.

The moment Alicia's eyes lock on the doll, she gasps.

"No way," she whispers.

"Yes way," I reply.

She steps out of the house and closes the screen door quietly behind her. Even now, my feelings are a little hurt that she doesn't invite me inside.

"It's impossible," she says. "How—"

"She was in my bed," I interrupt. My voice shakes. *She was under my covers!* Just the thought makes me shiver with disgust.

"But I checked my tin this morning," she says.

"Me, too. The ashes are still there."

She pauses. I hear her parents moving about in the house. Making coffee. Listening to swing on the radio. Being normal parents, as if this very strange and very scary event isn't even happening.

"Are you sure—" she begins.

I show her the writing on the doll's leg before she finishes.

"That's my handwriting," she says. She gulps.

I nod.

"What does this mean?" she asks.

"I don't know," I reply. I try to steel my voice. Try to sound assured. Even though, deep inside, I'm very much not. "But today, we're going to find out."

We run by James's house to loop him in and then

go straight back into town. I tell them all about my dreams as we walk.

"I don't think anyone has lived in that mansion for a long time," James says. "Are you sure they're not just bad dreams?"

His voice sounds dazed when he says it. Probably because we woke him up. His tone still creeps me out—he sounds way too much like an adult talking about the past.

"Even if they *are* bad dreams," I say, "it doesn't explain *this*." I shake the doll in front of him. He flinches back. "We have to find out what's going on. I need to know who lived in that mansion and what happened to them. And if anyone would know about the history of this town, it's the mayor."

James nods. It's clear he doesn't want to be here. It's clear the doll scares him.

Only Alicia seems excited. She practically beams as we hustle down the sidewalk, heading toward the mayor's house. Finally, she's getting a real adventure.

I don't quite know what I'm going to ask. I don't know what sort of answers Mayor Couch could give. All I know is that I need to have answers, since there's nothing I can do to make the doll leave me alone. Maybe learning about the girl named Elizabeth will help.

We knock politely on the mayor's front door. His house is probably the grandest in town, with huge Roman columns stretching up on the wraparound porch, but even his house shows signs of age and neglect. The white walls are stained with years of dirt, and the furniture we can see through the large windows is threadbare and dusty. It's the closest to the manor that any house in town comes. Especially mine.

Mayor Couch answers the door. He's wearing a long bathrobe and slippers, and his thin hair is all wispy on his head.

"Hello, children," he says. He glances behind us. "What are you doing here so early? And where are your parents?"

"We're here to ask you some questions," I say. Then I remember my manners. "I'm sorry for disturbing you so early. But they really can't wait."

"Oh, well," he mutters. He steps outside and closes the door behind him. "What seems to be the matter?"

My voice lodges in my throat. For some reason, telling an adult about this makes it all more *real*. It's no longer a scary story between us kids. It's a problem. One that needs an adult to solve it.

"It's about the manor house in the woods," Alicia says boldly. I look at her, suddenly proud that she is my friend. "We wanted to know who lived there, and what happened to them."

"Manor house?" Mayor Couch asks. I look back at him—his eyes are unfocused, and his voice takes on the same hazy tone as before. "There's no manor house in the woods."

My mouth drops.

"There is," I say. "We've played there."

"You shouldn't be playing in the woods. Bad things are out there."

"What kind of bad things?"

"I can't tell you." He doesn't sound angry or defensive—his voice is distant, like he isn't even sure what is out there, and that is why he can't speak of it.

"Why not?"

"I can't say."

"Bad things like this?" I ask. I hold the doll in front of him.

It seems to take him a moment to actually see the doll. When he does, his expression changes. He becomes almost . . . angry.

"What is *that*?" he asks.

"I don't know," I say. "But I think it comes from the manor. I think it belonged to a girl named Elizabeth—"

He snatches the doll from my hand.

"If this is your idea of a joke," he says, "I'm going to have to have a talk with your parents."

"It's not a joke!" I yell. Then I try to control my voice—my mom always taught me that the best way to argue a point is to be calm and collected. He *has* to believe us. He has to have some sort of answer. "Something strange is going on, Mayor Couch. And we're trying to get to the bottom of it. It has to do with the manor—I know it."

"*There is no manor*," he replies. His voice once more takes on a distant tone. "And there was no little girl named Elizabeth. I will hear no more of it, or of this doll, or of her thieving family."

He hands me the doll. I clutch it to my chest.

"Now, I suggest you three find a different game. One that doesn't involve the woods or the mine. And one that definitely doesn't involve dolls."

With that, he steps back inside and closes the door in our faces.

James flinches back from the door and bites his lip. "I guess that's it, then," he says.

Alicia looks at me sadly. "I'm sorry, Kimberly," she says. "He wasn't any help after all."

"But he was," I say. I turn and head toward the library.

I didn't mention anything about Elizabeth's family.

But Mayor Couch called them *thieving*.

Clearly, he knows something about the manor and the family who lived there.

And if he won't tell me anything more about them, I know precisely who—or *what*—will.

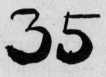

35

"Hello, Mr. Jones," I say when we step into the library.

It's warm and quiet in here, and the stacks smell like home.

"Hello, Miss Rice," he says. He peers at us over the top of his book, his eyebrows raised. "You've brought friends."

I feel myself blush. I don't think I've ever come in here with James and Alicia before; I can tell he's surprised that I have friends.

Then his eyes seem to catch on the doll and I can see his friendliness waver.

I quickly put the doll behind my back, introduce James and Alicia, and get down to business.

"I'm here for the book I returned yesterday," I say. I hesitate. "I, er, left my bookmark in it and it's very special to me."

For some reason, I don't want to tell him why we're looking for the book—after his and Mayor Couch's strange responses, I don't want to tell any other adults about what's going on. Especially adults who could hold the key to finding out the answer.

"Of course," he says. "Though I re-shelved it. Would you like me to help you find it?"

"That's okay, Mr. Jones," I say. "I remember where it is."

He nods and goes back to reading as though this is just a normal morning. I glance at my friends; my heart is racing, and I swear the doll is still cold to the touch. I wish I had a bag to stuff her in, but even then, I don't trust that she wouldn't escape and find some new way to terrorize me. If only she would move when others were looking; *then* people would believe me. They wouldn't have a choice.

Together, my friends and I rush to the back.

It doesn't take long to find the book. I hand the doll over to Alicia and use both hands to pull the large tome from the shelf. I don't know what I'm looking for, but I know the book will hold a secret. After all, it's the history of Copper Hollow—surely something like a mansion or a fire or even the copper mines will show up. If there was truly a rich family in town, they would have made the local history books.

We kneel down on the floor and I place the book between all of us. Carefully, I open the cover and flip to the table of contents.

It isn't there.

"What in the—" I whisper. I flip to the next page.

It, too, is blank.

Frustrated, my brain fuzzy, I begin flipping through the pages. How is the book blank? I remember reading it. And yet . . . for some reason, I can't remember a thing I read.

"Slow down!" James says. "You're flipping so fast that I can't read anything."

"What?" I ask. I let go of the pages. "What do you mean?"

"What do you mean, what do I mean?" He looks at me like I've lost it. "I can't read when you're flipping so fast."

"You can read this?" I say. I look back to the book. Blank. All the pages are blank. Looking at it makes my head hurt. "You can see words?"

"Um, Earth to Kimberly. It's a book. Of course I can see words. That's what books *are*."

Alicia doesn't say anything. She's watching me with a concerned look on her face, the doll still held tightly in front of her.

"But it's—" I begin. But I don't finish. Because the way they're both looking at me says it all: They can see words on the page, but I can't.

Suddenly, I'm reminded of the way Mayor Couch stared at the book, of the way an entire night seemed to pass by in a blur when I thought I'd read it. Something strange is happening.

I grab the nearest book from the shelf and pull it out.

It, too, is blank.

"No way," I mutter.

As if possessed, I yank the books from the bottom shelf, spilling them on the ground around us. All of them are blank. Every. Single. One.

Impossible.

"Kimberly, what are you—"

"What are you kids doing back there?" Mr. Jones calls out. I hear him slide his chair back—it squeaks against the granite floor.

I don't know what comes over me.

Maybe it's the panic of realizing that all the history books are blank. Maybe it's the shock that my friends aren't seeing the same things as me.

Or maybe it's the fear—the fear that I'm losing my mind, that I'm cursed.

The fear that this doll is ruining my life.

"Are you playing with us?" Alicia asks me.

"What?" I say. I sound too defensive.

"Are you saying you don't see any words on these pages?" she asks me.

I don't say anything. I don't understand why she sounds mad.

"Because there are words on these pages," she

continues. "And I don't understand why you'd say there weren't—unless this whole thing is a prank *you're* playing."

"Alicia," James tries to stop her. But he also sounds confused.

"Is this one of your stories?" Alicia presses. "You had us thinking someone was playing a prank on you. But are you playing a prank on *us*?"

"No!" I say. Then again. "No."

But I'm not sure she believes me.

And then

      in my head

           I hear the doll laughing

              and I know Alicia doesn't

              and James doesn't.

I am the only one.

I am all alone in this, and I have no idea why.

I've stopped talking, and now Alicia is starting to think she's right.

The doll's laughter grows louder.

It fills the library.

It fills my head.

I am the only one who hears it.

I grab the doll and leap to my feet.

Before anyone can stop me, I run from the library. I don't stop.

I don't look back.

36

I make it all the way to the edge of town before I real-
ize where I'm going.

I'm leaving.

My feet push me down the dusty road that
stretches past the mine. I don't slow down when I
see it, even though my head swims with vertigo and
dream memories as I pass. All I can think of are my
friends' shocked expressions as I opened the blank
books. The anger in Alicia's eyes when she thought
this entire thing was one big prank I was playing on
them. I remember the way they looked at me when I
tried to go deeper into the mansion, the same glazed

expression as Mayor Couch had when I tried talking about the past.

I don't know what is going on in Copper Hollow. *Something* is wrong here. Something to do with the mine and the family that lived in the mansion and this stupid doll.

Something is wrong, and I don't want to have anything else to do with it.

So I keep running. Down the road and through the trees, their branches a rustling canopy above me. For some reason, I swear they sound like the laughter of the doll. I swear they're mocking me.

I run until I can't run anymore, until I'm out of breath and panting, one hand on my side and the other clutching the doll. I look ahead of me.

More forest. Just like behind.

Surely I should have hit something now? A highway or another road? I feel like I've been running for half an hour.

I look down at the doll.

"I'm going to get rid of you once and for all," I mutter. I look ahead. I'm going to take the doll and throw it on the highway and watch as a car runs it over. Or I'll toss it in the back of a truck and watch it drive away.

At least, I think there's a highway out there. There has to be, right? I've never actually seen one . . .

I finally gather my breath and begin walking—quickly—in the direction of Copper Hollow's only exit. Even if it takes all day, I'm getting out of here—and getting the doll out of here, too.

I keep expecting the sky to grow dark and crows to gather. Instead, the day stays cheery and hot, and after I've walked at least another twenty minutes I begin to think I should have brought water. I wonder if maybe I've made the wrong decision. Shouldn't there be cars? Shouldn't there be someone passing by?

But there's no one.

What if I get lost out here? Worse, what if my friends are back home looking for me? What if they think I'm hurt?

What if my mom is worried?

For some reason, I think of my dad.

He left down this very road, and he never came back.

Did my mom worry about him when he left? Did

he do it to find a better job so we could live a better life? Or did he abandon us?

My mom's never told me, and I've always been too scared to ask more. I don't want to upset her.

I wonder what he found down this road. The thought excites me, that I'll see what he saw. If only for a moment. Right before I toss the doll away and get her out of my life for good.

I keep walking.

The road twists. I can't see what lies beyond, and that makes me walk faster.

There has to be a highway out there. I'm almost free of the doll. She's almost out of Copper Hollow.

I turn the corner

and my heart drops.

I haven't escaped.

The road has led me straight back to the mansion.

37

Everything goes hazy.

My head spins and my knees wobble and shadows creep in at the corners of my vision. Along with a giggling that I know isn't entirely in my head.

In the past, the mansion filled me with wonder. Now it just fills me with dread.

I have to get out of here. I have to get rid of the doll.

I turn around—maybe if I go back the way I came I'll find the real exit. Maybe I just accidentally took the wrong path.

The mansion sits before me.

"No," I whisper.

Maybe I'm still dreaming. Maybe all of today has been one long nightmare and I will wake up soon.

I pinch myself. It stings. Nothing changes.

I squeeze my eyes shut and will myself to wake up, for all of this to go away. When I open them again, the mansion is still there. Broken and imposing and demanding my attention.

I turn around.

The mansion is there.

No matter which way I look, the mansion is in front of me.

I look down at the doll in my hand and receive another shock.

Her tiny arm is raised, and her finger points directly at the mansion.

"You want me to go in there?" I ask.

Very slowly, she nods.

I know I should scream, but at this point, too many strange things have happened for this to surprise me. I don't even drop her to the ground. I just swallow my fear and disbelief and stare up at the mansion that has always drawn me near.

It all adds up: the dreams, the strange reactions of the town and my friends. Even the doll.

Everything leads back here, to the mansion.

Everything leads back to a history that no one remembers.

I look back down to the doll and her dress. *BURY ME*. And then I know the answer:

She doesn't want me to bury her just anywhere.

She wants me to bury her here.

"Okay, then," I say to the doll and whatever ghosts are listening. "Let's put you to rest, once and for all."

38

This time, when I enter the mansion, I'm not playing make-believe.

I don't need to.

Not when a creepy doll is guiding me forward and every corner is thick with cobwebs and dream memories.

Not when I feel like I'm caught in a larger story, one that not even *my* imagination could create.

I honestly don't even know where I'm going. I let my feet guide me forward. Through the huge foyer, past the crumbling, curving staircase, down hallways filled with burned and toppled statues. The only sounds are the rustle of pigeons in the eaves and the ceramic crunching beneath my shoes. With every step, the air grows colder. The doll in my hand turns to ice. I know I should want to turn around and run away, but something about this feels . . . right. For some unknown reason, I feel like I am a part of this place, and now—finally—I'll find out why. After wandering down more hallways and past more rooms than I can count, after I am definitely one hundred percent lost and unable to find my way out, I find myself back in the grand ballroom.

Once more, my dream sweeps into focus, along with the suffocating claustrophobia of being surrounded by so many costumed dancers. I find myself clutching the doll to my chest and spinning on the spot, staring up at the burned window frames and walls with my breath caught in my throat.

Faintly, I hear the hum of orchestral music, the bubble of laughter. And then I hear the crackle of fire.

Phantom smoke fills my nostrils.

Shadows flicker in the corner of my eyes, shadows like twitching firelight.

I hear the laughter turn to screams.

Awe turns to panic as the screams and the smoke grow louder, as the music crashes, as the nightmare becomes a reality and I know if I stay in here I'll be burned alive.

I run.

I head toward the far end of the ballroom, down a narrow hall I know I've never ventured through before. Cobwebs smear over my face and knobs of wood tangle my feet, but I don't stop running. Not even as the air grows colder and the hallway tilts darker. Steps tumble down before me, and I take them two at a time, the hall lit by dim light filtering from behind.

It's only when the steps turn back into a hallway that the screaming stops. I slow. My breath comes out in heavy puffs as I try to calm down. I need to get out of here. But I know I'm not going to escape. Not until I've done what the doll wants me to do.

"You want me to bury you in here?" I ask in a whisper.

There's no answer, and I can't tell if that makes me feel better or worse. I still feel like I'm losing my mind; would hearing the doll's voice make that go away?

I know I need to bury the doll. The question is where. I don't want her coming back again. I don't want this weirdness getting worse.

It's then that my eyes adjust to the darkness. Everything in here is lit by the faint stream of broken light coming down the stairway behind me. I'm in a room—I can faintly see the walls, everything covered in black soot, the furniture nothing more than piles of ash. Everything black and shadowed.

Something glints.

On the other side of the room, a flash of gold.

Gold.

I take a step forward, and suddenly the room is filled with light. Like someone has flipped a switch, or lit a dozen lanterns, the room glows with warmth. Before my eyes, the room changes.

Soot and dust fade, floating up and disappearing like snow falling in reverse, revealing stone walls and intricate paintings. An accent table holding a vase of dried flowers materializes in front of me, but that's not what makes my breath catch.

On the other side of the room, locked behind a thick door of iron grating, is the treasury.

I look down at the doll. She is smiling.

I think I know where she wants to be buried.

39

I walk forward in a trance, my mind spinning.

This is the treasury where Elizabeth used to hide.
This is the room where she found the doll for the first
time. The question is, why is she bringing me here?
Why does the doll want to be buried in the basement?
Maybe she likes gold?

Or maybe . . . maybe she wants me to have this
treasure?

Just the thought makes my heart flip. I always
thought the doll was trying to harm me. But what if
she was trying to help me all this time?

My free hand wraps around the cool iron grate.

Beyond the bars, treasures beyond my wildest dreams glimmer with promise. Golden chalices covered in jewels, glittering pearls, shining candelabras, pyramids of silver bars, even an open chest overflowing with gold coins. How in the world did Elizabeth's family afford all of this?

And there, against the wall, is the painting that Elizabeth had hidden behind. There's a large scratch across it, but I can make out the two figures. Two men. One is her father, and the other . . . looks very familiar. Was he in the dream?

I know I have to get in there. The doll wants me to have this treasure. She wants me to have a better life, to escape from Copper Hollow with my mom and my friends. To escape just like my father did. I don't worry about why. That's not important.

I reach to open the door. It doesn't budge.

For a moment, disappointment floods me. I can't have come so far, only to be stopped by a locked door.

Something clanks to the ground at my feet.

The locket!

Somehow, it fell off the doll's neck. The force of the fall snapped the amulet open. And it wasn't empty. There, nestled inside, is a tiny skeleton key. And it looks like it's the perfect size for the lock.

With shaky hands, I pick it up and place it in the lock.

"Please work," I whisper to myself. "Please, please work."

I turn the key.

The lock opens, and I gasp a huge sigh of relief. Excitement races through me at the thought of suddenly having so much money.

I barely even notice setting the doll down as I step inside—my body is on autopilot, and everything I see glints gold.

My mom and I will be able to get a house. No, not just a house—a *mansion*. One even bigger than this. One so big that all of my friends will have their own wings. We'll be able to play hide-and-seek all day and still not visit every room. We'll hire a chef to cook all of our meals. I'll never have to eat ramen again, and my mom will never have to work behind a greasy stove. The thought is almost enough to bring me to tears.

Everything is finally going to be okay.

Better than okay. We'll go out there and find Dad and everything is going to be amazing now because I'm finally, magically, *rich*.

A creak behind me derails my thoughts.

I turn.

Just in time to see the door swinging closed.

I lunge for it

        but I'm too late.

The door shuts.

The lock clicks.

My excited daydreams shatter into a million pieces as a dark reality settles over me.

I push against the door, but it won't budge.

I look up to see the doll smiling at me from the other side of the bars.

I shake the door wildly.

It doesn't budge.

I am trapped. Alone. In the basement of an abandoned manor that no one seems to remember. And no one knows where I am.

The lights go out.

The giggling begins.

40

Darkness.

Pitch-black darkness. Not even sunlight from the hall.

It's so dark, I can't see my own hands, not even when I bump them into my nose.

I can't tell if the giggling that echoes around me is from miles away or right at my feet.

Something scurries past my legs. The giggling is for sure coming from at my feet.

I jerk away and press up against the door, the bars to my back.

"What do you want from me?" I yell out. My voice trembles.

The giggling just gets louder. Something rubs against my leg once more. A tiny doll hand.

Many tiny doll hands.

I scream as they claw at my ankles, as the laughter gets louder.

There's nowhere to run. No way to escape.

"Help me, somebody, please!" I yell. Maybe James and Alicia are out there. Maybe someone is close enough to hear me, to help me . . .

"No one is going to come for you," chides a girl's voice. "No matter how loud you scream, they'll never hear you. They never hear."

Instantly, the clambering and giggling stops. Instead, I hear a girl softly crying.

"Who . . . who are you?" I ask.

The voice is familiar, but I can't figure out why. It's not Alicia. It's not any girl from school. Wait, can it be . . . ?

"You know who I am, Kimberly Rice," the girl says. "Just as I know who you are."

Light flickers, pale blue and ethereal. And there, before me, hovers a young girl with curly hair, wearing a beautiful ball gown. The same gown I was wearing in my dreams. The same gown as the doll that led me here.

"Elizabeth," I gasp. "Are you . . . dead?"

The girl nods. Her eyes are darkened with sadness, and when she looks at me, my chest goes cold with despair.

"Indeed," she says. "And it is nice to finally meet you . . . cousin."

41

"Cousin?" I whisper.

My thoughts congeal like honey—nothing feels real, and yet I'm not waking up. Her words settle into my bones with a familiarity that feels awfully close to truth.

She nods.

"Your father and mine were brothers," she says. "But they did not act like brothers for very long." She looks down, her hair falling back over her face. "Perhaps it would be better to show you."

Glowing fog curls in her hand, swirling to form a ghostly doll, exactly the same as the one that's been haunting me. Only this one doesn't have words on its dress.

Elizabeth holds it out to me.

"It is time you know the truth," she says. "About Copper Hollow. About our family. And about our curse."

"Curse?" I whisper.

"Yes," she says gravely. "The curse I brought about."

Her eyes look so sad that even though she's just admitted to something terrible, I still feel pity for her.

"Okay," I whisper. I want to know. I reach out and touch the doll.

The moment my hand closes around its vaporous body, the darkness around me swirls white and fades.

"We were once the wealthiest family for miles around," Elizabeth's voice echoes.

The mansion soars around us. We stand out in the courtyard, birds singing in the warm summer air. Sunlight glitters off the many windows of the mansion and the plume of water from a nearby fountain—the very fountain James used only days ago as his make-believe crow's nest. The mansion is no longer crumbling and burned, but pure white, complete with window boxes overflowing with flowers. The gardens that were overrun with weeds spread out around us, green and vibrant and filled with roses and so many other flowers I couldn't begin to name them. It is beautiful and lavish, everything around me absolute perfection.

Which doesn't explain why Elizabeth sounds so sad when she speaks.

A young girl runs out in front of us, chasing a ball. It takes me a moment to realize it is a younger version of Elizabeth.

"When I was a child, I thought I was a princess," the ghost beside me says. "Playing every day in a castle built just for me. But as I grew older, I realized the truth: I wasn't a princess, and this wasn't my castle. I was a prisoner, and the mansion was my penitentiary."

The scene shifts, and we are suddenly following a slightly older version of Elizabeth along a hallway. Portraits of stern-looking family members glare down at her.

"I wasn't allowed to have friends," Elizabeth says

at my side. "My parents thought it was dangerous for me to socialize outside of our *class*. So I was left to my own devices, to play make-believe and pretend I was somewhere better . . . just like you."

She looks at me. For a moment, I can see the family resemblance, and I wonder if maybe she's telling the truth about us being related. But that can't be true. Mom would have told me about having a cousin and an amazing past, right?

"Eventually, though, even my imagination wasn't enough to hide me from the truth of my family's empire."

The scene shifts again, and we are now standing in the public square in downtown Copper Hollow. Over there is the library. And there, the police station. Everything looks exactly the same, so much so that I almost wonder if I've been transported out of the treasury.

Until I look over and see the crowd that's gathered.

Even from here, and even though I can't hear anything, I can tell the crowd is angry.

One man stands on a crate in front of them,

shouting and gesturing with his fist. The crowd mimics him, just as angry, just as ready for action. They are soot-covered, their clothes torn and dirty. Some look like people I know, but it's hard to tell from the grime on their faces. Something about the man on the crate tickles the back of my mind. He looks familiar, but how?

"The people of Copper Hollow were angry," Elizabeth says. "For years, my parents had been stealing from the very miners whose work brought them their wealth. They ran the city council and taxed the town heavily—in addition to keeping all of the profits from the mine. But people were too scared to do anything. They knew that if they spoke up, my family could close down the mine and everyone would be left without a job or food. That is the true reason my parents wouldn't let me leave my house—they didn't want me to see what monsters they were."

"Those people don't look scared," I say. "They look ready to attack."

"They are," she replies. "And they will. A week ago, a section of the mine collapsed, trapping and killing the workers inside. The rest of the miners knew the mines were unsafe, and they wanted my family to fix them before resuming work. My family refused and sent them back down, swearing that if production lessened, the town would pay for it dearly. That was the last straw. Their fear turned to anger, and that anger turned to action."

A sudden movement from a side street catches my eye. I look over to see a copy of Elizabeth standing in the shadows of a house, watching the group with a wide, scared expression.

"I snuck out of the house the day my family was holding a grand ball for all of their richest friends. Families from many towns over were to be attending. I didn't want to go, especially not after what I had seen. I almost didn't return home that night, but I feared being caught by the townspeople as much as I feared my parents' wrath."

She turns to me.

"I thought that it might be safer at home, anyway. Because no one from town was invited. Little did I know, they would show up anyway."

"What happened?"

"This is the night they burned down the mansion and murdered me and my family," Elizabeth says. My blood goes cold, but her next words freeze it in my veins. "And that man on the podium is the reason for it. That man . . . that man is your father."

42

"My father?"

Words barely form in my cloudy brain. I crumple to my knees, and in that moment, the scene shifts.

We are back in the mansion. Up on the balcony. Below us, the crowd of costumed dancers promenades and spins in silence.

"Yes," Elizabeth says. She kneels at my side. Her ghostly hand tingles cool and oddly comforting on my shoulder. "Though I suppose you would not remember."

"Why . . . I thought . . ." *I thought he ran away before I was born. I thought he was a nobody like me.*

"Your father was an angry man," Elizabeth says. "Even though he came from wealth, he and my father had a huge fight, and your father was cut off from the family and its luxury. He worked in the mines, and he never forgave my father. He eventually convinced the town to revolt. To tear down our manor and make our family pay. My parents knew of the threats, but they did not think he would follow through. They thought he would never betray his own blood like they had. But the night of the ball, he did."

Bricks shatter through the great stained glass windows at her words. Bricks wrapped in flaming paper. Instantly, the ballroom explodes into silent chaos. Flames lick up the satin curtains and spread through the ballroom, leaping across dresses and tuxedos. I watch in horror as the dancers try to escape, but their paths are barred—none of the doors leading from the ballroom will open.

"They blocked off all the exits when they attacked," Elizabeth says dully. "They didn't want to ruin just my family—they wanted to destroy anyone with a lick of wealth. There were no survivors."

The scene shifts again, disappearing in a whorl of smoke and flame.

We are now back in the treasury. Jewels and gold glimmer from every surface.

"I hid down here to escape long before the townspeople attacked. I wanted to hide from my parents and their friends and their terrible hypocrisy. To live with so much wealth while everyone else starved seemed like the most terrible thing. But I had no clue how I would get out. I wished with all my heart that I would be free of them. Free of my family and their monstrosity.

"I hadn't wanted this, though. I never would have wanted this."

Light flickers in the hallway. Light, and the unmistakable scent of smoke. A vision of Elizabeth peeks out from behind a painting to investigate.

"By the time I realized the mansion was on fire, it was too late."

Someone holding a torch runs down the steps. My chest constricts at the sight.

It's my father.

The vision of Elizabeth retreats back behind her painting.

"I didn't know what was going on. I only knew to hide. I didn't dare think of what your father would do if he found me. But he wasn't interested in me. He was only interested in what my family had stolen."

My father seems surprised to find that the treasury door is unlocked, but he doesn't hesitate. He rushes inside and fills his pockets with gold and jewels, hastily draping pearls over his neck. I watch in fear and disgust as he hurriedly stashes as many treasures as he can on his body. When he turns around, his eyes brush over me.

I swear he can see me.

The look in his eyes—the greed, the hatred—makes me cower away.

If this is my father, I'm glad he's gone.

Even in the vision, I hear the click of the door as it latches shut behind him and he races up the hall. Smoke billows down after him.

"I often wonder if he would have saved me, had he known I was there," Elizabeth muses. "But I do not think so. He was as much a monster as my parents. Perhaps more so. It doesn't matter, though. The damage was done."

Moments later, I watch speechlessly as the vision of Elizabeth rushes from her hiding space. She grabs at the door, the doll forgotten and splayed on the ground beside her. The door doesn't budge. The key glints ominously on the ground just out of her reach.

Smoke fills the room, thick and acrid. I cough at the same time Elizabeth does. I feel her panic, her fear. The hurt that someone would do this.

"I burned with the rest of the treasure," she says as smoke fills the vision and the present day returns. "My ghost has stayed here ever since, unable to leave, forever stuck in my prison. Until you, Kimberly. Now that you are here, I believe I am ready to forgive and move on and lift the curse." She looks at me, and her gaze is sharp.

"But first . . . I require that you help me."

43

"Curse?" I ask. "What do you mean, curse?"

Elizabeth sighs.

"Did you ever wonder why no one from Copper Hollow ever leaves?" she asks. "Or why you and your mother live on the outskirts, never able to know the warmth of a house?"

Her words make me shiver. I nod.

She continues, and her voice shifts to anger.

"When I was dying, I swore I would make this town pay. I put a curse on the town, that anyone living here would never be able to leave or move on with their lives—I wanted them to be as stuck as I felt. And I cursed my entire family, so those surviving would never know wealth again. But in doing that, I cursed myself. My rage kept my soul trapped here, unable to escape or forget. The town could not move on, but neither could I. Worse, my curse backfired; I was forced to live with the memory of what happened, but all traces of my family were wiped from the minds and histories of those who live here."

That explains the blank library books, and the fact that no one ever goes near or seems to remember the mansion, I think in wonder.

"But what about me?" I ask.

"I wanted to hate you for what my uncle—your father—did to me. And for years, I did. Especially when I realized that he had fled town right after stealing from us and managed to sneak off before my curse took hold. I wanted revenge. But then I watched you playing with your friends. Using your imagination just as I did to visualize a better world. You saw things no one else could, beauty where there was only pain. You weren't greedy like your father. Even after he left your family behind, you held on to hope that things could improve, and you worked hard to make that happen. It took time, but eventually I realized you weren't to blame for all this, and it was wrong of me to make you suffer. You started to see the truth of the town, and my mansion. When I knew you were ready, I sent you the doll so you would find me."

I look down at the doll still standing on the other side of the door. Only days ago, she felt like a curse. Could it be that she was actually the key to breaking one?

"What can I do?" I ask. "I've never known my dad. If you need me to get your jewels back, I can't help you."

For the first time since I've known her, Elizabeth smiles. Even then, it is still sad.

"I have no need for gold or jewels. No, I want this town to finally face what they did and for my story to finally be told. And you, who are such a good story-teller, are the one to do it."

44

Later that evening, I have Mayor Couch call a town meeting.

I don't expect him to believe me or follow through, but when I show him the piece of gold that Elizabeth gave me and tell him it has to do with the mine, he agrees. Maybe it's linked to the curse. Or maybe he's just greedy for more gold. I hope it's the former.

So there we stand, Mayor Couch and me, in the town hall in front of the entire town. Even my mom is there, sitting in the front row right beside Alicia and James. They all look up at me with very confused expressions on their faces.

Mayor Couch clears his throat. The buzz of chatter dies down.

"Our very own Kimberly Rice wanted to speak with you all tonight," Mayor Couch says. "I'm not certain what it's about, but I have good reason to believe it's very important. To all of us. Kimberly?"

I feel like all the spotlights in the world have been turned on and pointed straight at me. All the blood rushes to my cheeks, and my hands instantly grow sweaty.

I step forward and try to hold my head high.

I've been telling stories my entire life.

When I hold the gold out and hear a murmur ripple through the crowd, followed by a hushed silence, I know this is the most important story I will ever tell.

45

"Elizabeth?" I call out.

I creep down the steps of the abandoned mansion. Night has fallen, and the lantern in my hand casts sharp lines and shadows over the debris. Gold glitters amidst the destruction. All the gold in the treasury is still there, just melted. All of this is—technically— my family's. Mine.

"Did you tell them?" I hear in response.

She swirls to life in front of me, pulled from a blue fog like a flame.

I nod.

"I told them everything. About the mansion, and the fire, and the curse."

"Did you mention the gold?"

I nod again.

"I told them that we didn't need to suffer in poverty anymore. That the town was now rich. And I will make sure that everyone gets their fair share."

Elizabeth looks confused.

"But the gold is yours," she says. "It belongs to the Rice family. You could have kept it for yourself— the curse would be lifted even if you only told my story."

"I know," I reply. "But I didn't want to be greedy. Not after what greed has done to our family and this town. Fair is fair. I want all of us to have a better start."

Her confusion turns into a smile of relief.

"I knew you were the right one," she says. "I knew you would help end this nightmare."

"Is that it, then? Is the curse broken?"

There was a heavy silence after I'd shared Elizabeth's story with the crowd. I remember looking at my mother and seeing tears in her eyes—it was only when she hugged me after the meeting that she said she finally remembered my father and what had happened. She had stayed behind that night because of the pregnancy. She remembered, and she believed, and it seemed like everyone else had a similar experience. Mayor Couch was red-cheeked, and he apologized to me personally, as he had been one of the townspeople who lit the manor ablaze. Even Mr. Jones the librarian came up to me after to say sorry for not protecting the town's history like he had meant to.

Only James and Alicia remained stoic.

"We always knew something was strange," Alicia said. "Just as we knew you'd be the one to solve it."

I didn't know if she was telling the truth entirely, but I didn't really care. It was good to know my friends believed and supported me.

"The curse isn't over yet," Elizabeth says, drawing me back to the present. "Not entirely. There is still one more thing you must do."

She bends over and picks up the doll from the

ground. It's then that I see the bones poking up from the ash.

"What do you need me to do?" I ask.

"Exactly what I asked you to do from the very beginning."

She holds the doll out to me, and I read the words on its dress.

I nod.

Finally, I know precisely what she needs me to do, and what she had been trying to tell me all along.

Epilogue

I'm leaving Copper Hollow.

I want to.

Even though I have my imagination, I know there is a bigger world out there. One that isn't made up of cursed treasures and haunted dolls. And I am going to find it.

I look over at my mother, who smiles at me from the driver's seat of our new car. Our scant luggage is in the back seat, beside a duffel bag filled with gold—gold that I found tucked safe in my bed. A tiny note rested atop it, in the same handwriting as on the doll's dress.

DON'T BURY THIS.

Both Alicia and James are moving to the same new city as we are. We will be neighbors. We'll live in nice houses and play with new kids, and learn new games, and tell new stories. I don't know if we'll look for my father. I don't know if I want to.

All I know is, we are finally free of this cursed town. We have a future. We are safe. Everyone can move forward.

I smile and settle into my seat. Finally, we are leaving all of this behind. Stepping into something new.

As I watch the town copper mine disappear behind me, I feel a sense of contentment bubble up in my chest. With the curse lifted and Elizabeth and her doll laid to rest, we can all finally move on with our lives and be better people.

My eyes flutter closed. It's over. Finally over.

But when I glance at the side-view mirror, I see something shifting through the trees. Many things.

Dolls. Dozens of them. Wearing ball gowns or tuxedos, just the same as all the dancers I saw in the ballroom that fatal night.

And on each of their outfits are two words:

BURY ME

About the Author

K. R. Alexander is the pseudonym for author Alex R. Kahler.

As K. R., he writes creepy middle grade books for brave young readers. As Alex—his actual first name—he writes fantasy novels for adults and teens. In both cases, he loves writing fiction drawn from true life experiences. (But this book can't be real . . . can it?)

Alex has traveled the world collecting strange and fascinating tales, from the misty moors of Scotland to the humid jungles of Hawaii. He is always on the move, as he believes there is much more to life than what meets the eye.

You can learn more about his travels and other books, including *The Collector, The Fear Zone,* and the other books in the Scare Me series, on his website: cursedlibrary.com

He looks forward to scaring you again . . . soon.

Be afraid. Be very afraid.
K. R. Alexander's latest is
coming to haunt you.

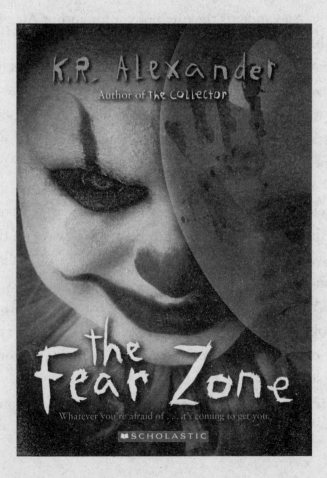

April

"Hey, give that back!" I yelp.

Andres grins, which looks really creepy since he's wearing fake vampire fangs for Halloween. He doesn't hand back the folded piece of orange paper he's snatched from my locker—instead he takes a step back and waves it while other costumed kids walk down the hall around us. He's been my best friend since sixth grade, and even now, two years later, he sometimes acts like my little brother. My very annoying little brother.

Andres starts opening the folded letter.

"Come on, give it back."

Andres shakes his head, still smiling, unfolding the note slowly.

Honestly, I have no idea what the note is, and I don't want Andres to be the first to find out. Maybe it's from a friend telling me about a last-minute Halloween party. Or maybe it's from my archnemesis, Caroline, telling me I look ugly in my black cat costume. It wouldn't surprise me. She's gone from good friend to enemy ever since last year.

I feebly snatch at the paper one more time, but Andres dances back a step. The page is almost entirely unfolded now.

He reads it to himself. His smile slips.

"What is this?" he asks. "Some sort of joke?"

He turns the paper over, and I read what's written in messy paint on the other side.

MEET IN THE GRAVEYARD. TONIGHT. MIDNIGHT. OR ELSE.

"Huh?" I ask. I grab for the paper again. This time he lets me have it. "Who wrote this?"

Andres shrugs and leans against the locker beside mine.

"Maybe it's a prank?" he says.

I keep rereading the note. I don't recognize the handwriting. It's not Caroline's, that's for sure. I don't think I have any other enemies at Jackson Middle School.

Do I?

I want to crumple up the letter, but when I look at it again, chills race down my spine. Those two words: *Or else*.

Or else *what*?

"It has to be a prank," I reply. "A Halloween scare. I bet some kids from the high school are going to be there to scare us or something."

It wouldn't surprise me. Kids in our town love Halloween, and I've heard a bunch of stories about high school kids taking the scares too far. Dressing up as monsters and running after little kids. Throwing pumpkins on cars. Apparently, years ago, a kid even went missing while playing hide-and-seek in the graveyard, and wasn't found until the next morning.

I shudder and crumple the note, tossing it in a

nearby trash can. Whatever this is, I don't want any part in it.

"Come on," I say. I shut my locker and zip up my bag. "Let's go. I think Mom finally brought all the Halloween candy out of hiding."

"You had me at *candy*," Andres says. He takes my arm, and together we walk down the hall and out of the school. But no matter how loudly we talk about other things, I'm haunted by the feeling:

Someone wants me to be at the graveyard.

At midnight.

Someone wants me to be afraid.